Dare to Dream Again

a Sweet Dreams Christian Romance by Alana Terry

To my mother, Gloria.

I'm so sorry we didn't have more time together before God took you home, but I'd like to think that you'd be proud of this novel.

Note: The views of the characters in this novel do not necessarily reflect the views of the author, nor is their behavior necessarily being condoned.

www.alanaterry.com

CHAPTER 1

I've never been so in love before.

Not like this.

He leans over as he takes my hand. So gentle, charming as he asks, "Would you care to do the honors and bless our meal?"

"Of course." I close my eyes but can still feel his gaze warming my face. I can't pretend not to notice. "Why are you looking at me like that?"

"You know." His voice is soft like the spring breeze that floats past. All around me, the smell of our cut grass is even stronger than the nasturtiums I just planted. He's worked hard. We both have.

Which is what makes this evening picnic a perfect way to end the day. Together. We couldn't ask for anything else.

He brushes my cheek with his work-worn finger. His callouses are surer signs of love than the smoothest, silkiest hand of royalty. "I'm sorry for distracting you," he says and shuts his eyes. "Go ahead."

Our fingers intertwine as I thank the Lord for our food, for our lives together. For all the sorrow he's brought us through and all the hope we have for our future. I thank him that he's given us two beautiful children. And as much as I love them and the way they cling to me through the day, I'm even more grateful that right now they are both fast asleep so we can enjoy this moment of peaceful stillness together.

"Amen." He leans over me. His breath is hot on my neck. "I love you," he says, but I can't say it back. My throat is clenched tight. My face is hot with tears.

What's wrong with me?

"I love you," he repeats, a question in his voice,

and more than anything I want to tell him the same.

Why can't I speak?

We have our daughters, we have the Lord, we have each other.

So why does it feel like my heart's been split in two? Why are these hot tears streaming down my cheeks?

Why is my husband's image disappearing in front of my eyes?

I love you too, but by the time I manage to whisper the words, he's gone.

It's only me.

Alone in the dark.

Stifling my cry so I don't wake up my teenage daughters.

Begging God for just five more minutes.

Five more minutes with my Stan.

Five more minutes where I can imagine we're together again.

No, not that long? What about sixty seconds? Ten seconds.

One …

I squeeze my eyes shut. It's hours before dawn, but I know I won't be able to get back to sleep.

I sit up in bed, turn on my lamp, and pick up my Bible, reminding myself that God blesses those who mourn no matter how hard it feels right now to believe those words.

CHAPTER 2

Gloria's alarm woke her up shortly after six, only an hour or so after she'd finally managed to get herself back to sleep. Dreams about Stan had become more and more common since their daughter's high school graduation last year. Memories that threatened to crush and overwhelm her.

The funny thing was that if Stan were still alive, she probably would have forgotten all about that picnic in the backyard. She wouldn't cling to those ridiculously mundane details of the four short years they'd had together. Making cream cheese and cucumber sandwiches to enjoy together that early summer evening. How many years ago?

Far too long.

She glided into her slippers, knowing that if she tried to hold her devotions in bed, she'd fall asleep again. At least her morning rituals were one part of her life where she felt she could be in complete control.

Tying her robe around her waist, she walked softly down the hall, careful not to make too much noise. She turned on the water for tea and sat down in her rocking chair, prayer journal in hand.

Well, Lord, I might be tired, but I'm ready to praise you today.

The morning would be a little more rushed than usual. Gloria would have to leave the house by 8:30 to get to the church on time. This would be her eleventh year making snacks for vacation Bible school. She'd been planning for weeks already, writing out shopping lists, pouring through old recipe books, testing new ideas in her kitchen.

This year would be different. Valley Tabernacle, the church across the river, was joining forces with

Orchard Grove Bible Church. It made sense. With only two congregations in a town this small, there was no reason for each church to hold a separate VBS when they could pool their resources and work together. At least that's what everyone had thought last spring when they started making plans. Gloria wasn't too thrilled about having to cook in someone else's space. She'd spent so much time at Orchard Grove Bible's downstairs kitchen that it felt like she owned the space. She hoped that with the venue changed to Valley Tabernacle's larger and newer campus she wouldn't feel like a guest intruding in on someone else's territory.

And so she prayed. About the kitchen, the children coming to VBS, the other volunteers helping out. Gloria had recruited her daughter Susannah to help her in the kitchen, as well as one of the young men who'd grown up at Orchard Grove, Ricky Fields. Now there was a boy who needed her prayers. Prayers that he would one day find the courage to tell Susannah how he truly felt about her. If they weren't a match made in heaven, Gloria didn't know who was. They'd practically grown up wearing the same diapers. Aside from being so shy, he was perfect for her daughter, and Gloria had no problem telling God so while she prayed over her day.

Once her tea was ready, she scooped in a small dollop of honey and took her mug back to the chair. This time of day was perfect. The girls were still asleep but not the birds outside. Birds who made for their Creator the glorious music that made everything look and feel peaceful and serene.

Oh, Stan. Remember those mornings together? When we woke up early before you went off to work? I'm sorry I didn't keep that up once the babies came. I should have found the energy to wake up with you even then. I had no idea how little time we'd have together. I miss you so much. If only you could see how beautiful the girls have grown up to be.

But of course, her husband didn't answer, and she was left to finish off her cup of tea alone.

CHAPTER 3

Gloria had only set foot in Valley Tabernacle twice, once for a wedding and once for a funeral, both times for individuals she'd hardly known. It was silly, but she felt the smallest wave of superstition sweep over her. Of course, the fine folks who attended Valley Tabernacle were just as much Christians as she was, but there were certain issues of both doctrine and practice that would make her more than a little uncomfortable to attend a service here.

It wasn't just the music, either. It was the entire style of worship. The loud, flamboyant *amens* and *hallelujahs* shouted out randomly from the congregation. The disorderliness of it all ... It was probably just prejudice on her part, but she was glad that her daughter and Ricky Fields had agreed to help out with snacks. Glad that she'd have volunteers she knew.

Of course, with her younger daughter Kitty having the health issues that she did, it was hard for both Gloria and Susannah to be gone from the house at the same time. That's why she was so thankful Ricky's mom agreed to spend the mornings with Kitty, who had required round-the-clock care her entire life. Yet another reason Gloria hoped Susannah and Ricky would get along well this week. Susannah had her heart set on becoming a missionary, but Ricky grew up here and was already being primed to take over his dad's courier business when he retired. A boy like Ricky could offer Susannah a nice, comfortable home right here in Orchard Grove.

Did you hear that, God? she joked as she found her way to the Valley Tabernacle kitchen. *Just give Ricky and Susannah one good week together.*

Please. That's all I ask.

"Good morning, Mrs. Peters. How are you doing today?"

Gloria smiled at the young boy she'd watched grow up since the first day he'd come to church all swaddled up like a baby burrito. Ricky's mom and Gloria had shared their first pregnancies together. Ricky was born exactly two weeks — almost to the hour — before Susannah. For years, the women had joked about their children growing up and falling in love. Now, Gloria hoped that God might remember their teasing and bring his good plans about for her daughter. If only Susannah would stop talking so much about wanting to run off to do mission work on foreign soil.

"Hello, Ricky." She wiped her hands on an apron she'd borrowed from the Valley Tabernacle closet. Reaching out to give him a small hug, she added, "I'm so glad you're willing to help out this week."

He cleared his throat. This summer he'd shot up at least half a foot, a second or late adolescence of sorts. Had Susannah noticed?

"How can I help?" Ricky asked.

Gloria peered over his shoulder, which was quite a bit broader than it had been just a year ago when he and Susannah graduated high school. "Oh, there's plenty to do," she answered, "but where's Susannah? Didn't she come with you?"

The schedule for the week worked out perfectly, at least in theory. Gloria would come to church early to get the kitchen set up. Ricky would drive over to the house to pick up Susannah and drop off his mom who had volunteered to sit with Kitty during the mornings, a huge blessing since she was one of the few people outside of family who could be trusted to take care of Kitty. It was a lot to ask of her, but Gloria wondered if she agreed so readily to play nurse all week because it would get Ricky and Susannah together in the same room for three and a half hours a day.

She eyed Ricky Fields, recalling how awkward and gangly he'd been just a few years earlier. No wonder Susannah had hardly paid him any attention. But now … Sure, he was still a little shy, but hopefully this week her daughter would realize how much her childhood friend had matured. Ricky was a fine young man.

Someone who would be good to her, provide for her, and never, ever take her away from Orchard Grove.

CHAPTER 4

"There you are, sweetie." Gloria leaned in to give Susannah an air hug since her hands were covered in flour.

"Smells good," Susannah said. "What are you making?"

Gloria was nodding subtly toward Ricky, hoping her daughter would take the hint and acknowledge him as well. That was the problem. Those two had grown up so close together they were just like siblings. Ricky was invisible to Susannah like the vase or photo you pass every single day until you stop noticing it at all.

Gloria had to snap her focus back onto her cooking if she wanted to have these snacks ready for the VBS students, who right now were upstairs screaming as loudly as they could, spurred on no doubt by the opening speaker.

She glanced at the pile of tablecloths she'd brought over from Orchard Grove Bible Church. "Why don't you two start setting the tables. I was hoping they'd be up for us by now, but I guess the folks here had other matters to worry about."

She nodded at some stacked folding tables against the wall. "Ricky, I don't think Susannah's strong enough to get those by herself. Why don't you help her out?"

Susannah led the way to the tables. Gloria wanted to call after her, whisper to her that she should let Ricky go first. Make him feel respected as a man. But those lessons could come later. All Susannah needed was for God to open her eyes to the potential residing in Ricky Fields. With the right kind of woman by his side, he could turn into one of the most upstanding citizens Orchard Grove had seen in decades.

Stan would have been so happy. As much as he jokingly complained about Gloria playing matchmaker while the kids were still young enough to swim naked together in the kiddie pool, he would be proud of the man Ricky had become.

Proud to make him his son-in-law.

It was supposed to get easier, wasn't it? When Gloria was a young widow struggling to raise a precocious preschooler and a toddler who failed to meet any of her physical or developmental milestones, she'd figured that by this point in her life, she'd have moved past the mourning stage. Her biggest worries back then were how to raise her daughters without their father leading her and offering his guidance, but with the Lord's help and a significant amount of heavenly grace, she'd managed.

"Here, Susannah. Let me get that for you." Ricky bumped his knee into one of the chairs, toppling it over, while he scrambled to grab and unfold the legs.

Gloria glanced at the pair surreptitiously and thought of God's many blessings.

Susannah had graduated a year early and was working now as a caretaker at an assisted living home. Kitty's condition was as stable as it ever would be. Both girls loved each other and loved the Lord. What more could she ask for?

A happy marriage for Susannah. A marriage as joyful and harmonious as Gloria and Stan's had been.

Yes. That's what she wanted for her daughter. That's why she was so anxious for this week to go perfectly for the two of them.

"What are you doing with those tables?"

Gloria snapped her head up from the cookies she'd been icing. Wiping her hands on her apron, she hurried out of the kitchen. "Can I help you?"

A slightly bald man in gym shorts and a sweat-stained T-shirt stood in the middle of the room. "What's going on?"

She didn't recognize him. Must be a member at

Valley Tabernacle. His name tag just said *Derek,* no last name. Gloria could only guess why he was bothering her now. She was already behind schedule. "Well, the snack tables weren't arranged, so I asked my daughter and her friend to set them up for us." She glanced at the clock on the wall. "The kids will be here in fifteen minutes." It wasn't much time to get things ready. She still needed to finish icing the cookies and then arrange the fruit in the shape of a dolphin to go along with the week's underwater theme.

Derek glanced around the room. "*My* kids'll be here in fifteen, you mean."

Gloria crossed her arms. "I beg your pardon?"

"This room is reserved for games and rec. Didn't you get the handout at the meeting?"

"I told Joy we needed this space to feed the kids, and she said it was all mine."

He shrugged. "Well, I checked again just this morning. Games and rec in the fellowship hall. We'll need these tables folded back up against the walls. I can help if you ..."

Susannah laid a gentle, placating hand on Gloria's shoulder, but Gloria ignored her. "And where do you expect the kids to eat all this food I've made?"

Another shrug. "Outside, like it says here on the schedule?"

As if he couldn't just as easily take his games and rec outside. Who needed an entire fellowship hall just to play duck, duck, goose?

She shook her head. "We've been planning on using the fellowship hall for weeks. Joy said it was ours."

"I'm sorry for the mix-up." There was a softness in his tone that for a second made her believe he meant it. "I can talk to Joy later, but for now I wonder if we better stick to what's printed." He pointed to a piece of paper taped to the wall.

Gloria didn't bother walking all the way over to read it.

"So what do you want to do?" Derek asked. "I

suppose we could squeeze the tables in over here and share the space."

She shook her head. Her kids would have no peace or quiet to eat their snacks with rowdy games and relay races going on just a few feet away. The last thing she needed was for a basketball to come crashing down on her fruit dolphin or a dodge ball to knock over one of the pitchers of lemonade.

She let out her breath in a loud huff that she hoped communicated her displeasure. "Well, if we just have to take the snacks outside, so be it. Good thing it's sunny."

He frowned and for a moment looked genuinely sincere. "Well, the kids aren't here yet. Will you at least let me help you take the food outside?"

She turned on her heel. "I'm sure we'll manage just fine by ourselves, thank you very much."

CHAPTER 5

"It's ok, Mom. It's really not a big deal." Susannah's voice was gentle and soothing as she and Gloria carried one of the folding tables outside. Ricky trailed behind them with the fruit platter.

"Look." Susannah smiled when they stepped outside. "It's gorgeous out. I really think we're getting the better end of the deal."

She sighed at her daughter's words. The first class was already here, running haphazardly across the lawn while they waited for Gloria to finish setting up.

Good thing the town wasn't supposed to get any rain. Heaven knew the orchards nearby needed it, but since the kids were relegated to eating their snacks outside, at least they wouldn't get drenched. She shook her head. Joy Holmes was one of the young mothers at Orchard Grove, a few years older than Susannah, and she'd volunteered to run VBS this year. Or more likely, she'd been elected to do so, which was the most common way for anything to get done at a church run by committees and subcommittees.

Joy had strong organizational skills, but she had so much else on her plate. Three young kids, plus her family had just moved into a larger house in the Orchard Heights area. She made hand-bound journals to sell at the Safe Anchorage gift shop, and to top it off, she had some sort of business/hobby as an online blogger. All that to say she had a very full schedule already even without the commitment of running vacation Bible school.

It was understandable for a mix-up like this to happen.

It shouldn't be that big of a deal.

"Mrs. Peters, where's the food?"

"I need to go potty."

"Teacher, Bowman just called me a baby."

"I did not."

"You did too."

Gloria clapped her hands to get everyone's attention. That was the problem being outside. Her voice didn't carry as far, and the children thought that they had free reign over the entire lawn.

"Hey, everybody!" Ricky shouted in a cartoon-style voice, and surprisingly the kids turned to gawk at him. "Listen up," he added then turned to Gloria who shot him a grateful look.

She reminded herself of all the reasons she loved working with kids this age. They were so impressionable, so hungry for love and eager to please. "Hello, class. Welcome to VBS."

A somewhat chubby boy with skinned knees crossed his arms. "You don't have to welcome us, you know. We've already been here like five hours."

Ricky knelt down next to him. "Hey, buddy.

What's your name?"

He glanced at Ricky as if sizing up an opponent. "Bowman."

"Bowman," Ricky repeated. "Well, listen, Bowman. Mrs. Peters is going to be your snack leader today, so if you want any of her special treats, you need to give her all your attention, all right?"

Bowman didn't reply, and Gloria did her best to remember everything she wanted to say. "Yes, well, for those of you who didn't hear, I'm Mrs. Peters. My daughter and her good friend are going to come around now and help all of you clean your hands. Then we're going to have a little Bible story before we eat."

Bowman picked up a stick from the ground and poked a hole in the grass. "We already listened to a Bible story in our other class. Why we got to do it all over again?"

Gloria glanced at the young boy's name tag. *Bowman Campos.* She didn't recognize the last name. Was he from Valley Tabernacle? Or maybe one of the neighborhood kids. All she knew was that if she were his mother, she would have taught him better manners. She was trying to think of what to say when Ricky jumped in.

"You know what, bud? The Bible's full of all kinds of great stories. And I bet you probably haven't heard them all, so let's give Mrs. Peters our full attention, ok?"

Bowman huffed and tried poking his neighbor one more time before Ricky took the stick from him. Gloria glanced at her daughter. Did Susannah notice how good Ricky was with the kids? Or was she too busy passing out the snacks to pay attention?

Once the kids got their food, things calmed down enough that Gloria could hear herself think. It was a pity they couldn't use the cute table decorations Gloria had spent so much time putting together. Most of the kids just sat down on the lawn. It would take a miracle to keep them all from getting stained. After the day was over, she'd go and talk to Joy. She hated to complain, but this was ridiculous. When

Orchard Grove Bible Church hosted VBS, games were always on the lawn. Obviously, that's what her kids wanted to do outside — play and run, not sit still in tidy little rows listening to her talk about the way Jesus fed the crowds with five loaves and two fish.

Then again, she'd learned at functions like these how important it was to be flexible. Wasn't she always complaining to herself about those stick-in-the-mud types at the church business meetings, the ones who never wanted to change and always had to have things done their way?

She'd been rude to Derek, which hadn't been fair of her either. It wasn't his fault that Joy had forgotten to switch the rooms.

She watched as two girls fought over whose cookie had the prettiest ocean wave icing before they both shoved their beautiful snacks into their mouths. Well, as long as the kids got fed, maybe that's what mattered most.

More flexibility. If there was one thing in life

Gloria prized, it was order. But she'd give it a try.

A little boy started to cry when Bowman stole his half of a banana. Gloria hurried over to make peace.

As long as she stayed this busy, she wouldn't have time to worry about where she was serving snacks.

And maybe she'd learn a little flexibility after all.

CHAPTER 6

"I'm going to head home with Ricky, Mom. Do you want me to carry anything out?"

Gloria smiled at her daughter. "No, sweetie. I need to dry these last few things, and then I'll be right behind you. The two of you take your time. I'll see you at home pretty soon." She kissed Susannah's cheek and whispered, "If Ricky wants to take you out for lunch or anything, you have my blessing."

She thought she detected the hint of a blush brighten her daughter's face but didn't want to get her hopes too high. She knew that once Susannah realized what a great boy Ricky really was that she'd fall as hard for him as Gloria had fallen for her dad so many years ago. Until then, she just had to be patient and wait for God to do his work.

Susannah was nothing like her mother at that age. Gloria had been headstrong, boy-crazy, and even a tad rebellious. Susannah, on the other hand, was as docile as a lamb, wanting nothing more than to move overseas and spread God's word. Sometimes Gloria worried about her. Had all of Kitty's health problems robbed Susannah of the childhood she should have had? Made her grow up too fast, too soon? Gloria had tried. She'd worked herself ragged taking Susannah to gymnastics and dance and art classes on top of all of Kitty's doctor and therapy appointments. But Susannah liked staying home. She liked tending to her sister. As she got older and Kitty's care got more complicated, Gloria was thankful for her daughter's help.

But she still felt guilty. How much of Susannah's childhood had been spent by the bedside of her chronically ill sister?

She glanced at the time, wondering if Ricky

would find the courage to ask her daughter out. If Gloria had been back at her own church kitchen, she would have finished up by now, but as it was, she spent twice as much time figuring out where the clean dishes should go than she did actually washing and drying them.

"So you made it through the first day."

Gloria looked up. There was that man again. Derek, the games and rec guy, only now his T-shirt was even more sweat drenched. With the temperatures as hot as they'd been this summer, had he really thought it'd be a good idea to wear gray?

"Can I give you a hand?" he asked.

She didn't meet his gaze. If Gloria had been able to serve the kids in the fellowship hall like she'd planned, she could have been twice as efficient with her time, cleaning up as the morning went on instead of letting all these dishes pile up to take care of at the end of the day.

"I think I can manage." She opened up three different cupboards and still couldn't find one spacious enough to hold the big mixing bowl. Everything was so haphazard at this church. She missed the nice, orderly kitchen at Orchard Grove Bible, with its labeled cupboards and shelves.

"Here." He took the mixing bowl out of her hands and opened up a cabinet above the fridge. "Don't ask me why they put it up here so high." He smiled.

Gloria mumbled her thanks. It was a smaller kitchen than she was used to working in, and it was inconvenient having to walk around someone else, but with Derek's help, they got the rest of the dishes put away in just a few minutes.

"Well." He placed his hands on his hips and looked around. "Looks pretty good in here."

"Yeah, thanks for your help." She gave him a smile. No reason to appear rude.

"Hey, it's supposed to be good weather all week. Why don't we switch off? I had the fellowship hall today. Why don't I let you use it tomorrow?"

Let her use it? Apparently he thought he was

being generous, having no idea that the first thing Gloria planned to do after cleaning up was find Joy and tell her that she'd need the fellowship hall for snacks for the rest of the week.

She let out her breath. "All right." At least it was a start. "Thanks." She'd use the fellowship hall tomorrow, and she'd still find Joy and make sure the room stayed hers for the remainder of VBS.

CHAPTER 7

"Did you have a nice time this morning, sweetheart?" Gloria asked Susannah as they worked together to get Kitty in her wheelchair for her afternoon snack.

"Yeah. It was quite a few kids, wasn't it?"

"Fifty-seven," Gloria answered. Not a bad turnout for a town this size. And quite a few more than Orchard Grove Bible Church brought in previous years when they did the VBS on their own.

"That's a lot of snacks," Susannah remarked. It was true. Gloria was tired after her long first day, but she didn't mind. She'd been cooking and baking for nearly as long as she could remember. After Stan died, during the years when the girls were little and

Gloria was certain she was messing everything up, baking remained the one thing she could always do well.

Didn't everyone need that one thing in their life? That one thing they could excel at no matter how poorly everything else might be going? She glanced at her daughters. Kitty, in spite of her health setbacks due to the cerebral palsy, excelled at making people smile, and Susannah excelled at nurturing others, which made her job at the Winter Grove assisted living home perfect for someone like her, someone with that gift of compassion.

Gloria was efficient and organized, but Susannah was truly an angel of mercy. Sometimes her daughter put her to shame by having more patience with Kitty's care than Gloria did herself. Susannah wanted nothing more than to spend her life watching over others, whether orphans in India or residents at the assisted living home or her sister right here. And hopefully soon, God would give her a husband and a family of her own, a family that she would love and nurture with that gentle spirit of hers.

"Did you have a good talk with Ricky on the drive home?" She tried to ask the question without attaching any special significance to it, but if the way Susannah's body stiffened was any indication, she didn't do that great of a job.

"You know Ricky," Susannah answered. "He's really quiet."

Kitty, who always loved when the conversation turned to Ricky Fields, let out a giggle and kicked her leg.

"Calm down," Gloria told her, perhaps more sternly than she'd needed. If Kitty went rigid, it'd be nearly impossible to get her into her wheelchair. The conversation would have to wait.

Although sometimes Gloria couldn't shake the feeling that time was running out. Last year, she'd found a lump under her armpit. Two different mammograms and one biopsy later, and she was assured she was perfectly healthy, but she'd been fighting off the premonition lately that she wouldn't have as much time with her daughters as she'd once hoped.

Maybe it was because Gloria's mother had passed away the year she and Stan got married. Was that it? Was Gloria worried that she would follow in her mother's footsteps and die young?

It was probably nothing. Having a daughter with as complicated a health history as Kitty's would make any single parent worried. Afraid of leaving the daughter who needed her. Gloria was just being paranoid.

That would certainly explain why she was so eager to see Susannah and Ricky settled down. But you couldn't rush these things. She just had to be patient. Let Susannah discover in her own time what a fine young man Ricky Fields was.

Pray and let God take care of the rest. That's what she had to do.

"Ready to go on a ride?" Susannah asked Kitty as she and Gloria worked together to transfer her to the wheelchair.

"All right." Shoving thoughts of matchmaking aside, Gloria wheeled her daughter into the kitchen. "Come on, girls. Let's see what we can dig up for a snack."

CHAPTER 8

I'm sitting here with our daughters, so impressed with how well they've turned out.

You remember that temper our little Susannah used to have? Remember when she screamed so hard she started pulling out her hair when things wouldn't go her way? And we were nervous and wondered what kind of spitfire she'd become.

Stan, she's amazing. She's so mature, far more mature than her age. Maybe that's why she hasn't fallen for Ricky yet. Maybe he needs a couple more years to catch up to her. She always was an old soul, wasn't she? Even as a baby (at least when she wasn't screaming). And she's beautiful. She looks quite a bit like your sister did at that age, actually.

Same long, blonde hair. She's lucky she's modest because there are so many young men practically drooling over her, and she doesn't even notice.

And Kitty ... Remember how much we used to worry, especially before we got answers from the doctors? And even at that time, cerebral palsy was still a very mysterious condition. They've made so many medical advances since then. It makes me wonder what her life might have been like if she'd been born today. Did you know there are babies who come fifteen or sixteen weeks early but still grow up to be perfectly healthy? It's miraculous. And even for babies with brain injuries, they have special therapies now and things to help them.

Your little angel. *Remember? That's what you used to call her. And she is. You know, for a girl who can't talk, she has such an attitude. Not in a bad way, but such a full personality. I love her so much, Stan. And I'm so scared of leaving her alone one day. I know Susannah will be here to take care of her then, but ...*

I don't know why I'm being so morbid. You know, it won't be too much longer before our daughters are older than you were when God took you home. You were far too young. I hope it's not blasphemous for me to say that. I know God has his purposes and I know not even a sparrow can fall to the ground apart from his will, but that doesn't stop what happened to you — what happened to our family — from being a tragedy.

There have been so many questions I've wanted to ask you, Stan. Simple things. Like whether it's time to update the will again or if the one I made when the kids were younger is good enough. If I should have pushed our insurance company to pay for more therapy appointments. We stuck at it for years, but Kitty hated them. It stressed her out so much it ruined her digestion, and in the end I really don't know if it did anything for her. But then I hear people talking about those talking devices people with cerebral palsy can learn to use, and I wonder if she should have kept at it, even when it was hard.

I know I shouldn't talk to you like you're still here. I know that you're in heaven with the Lord and probably so content and enraptured you're not even thinking about us down here, or if you are, it's just an excitement for when we all get to be together again. But I'm still here, still having to make all these tiny decisions (and big ones) that we should be making together.

Susannah's getting older, and I worry about her future. What if something happens to me, Stan? What if she has to put her entire life on hold to take care of Kitty? What if she grows resentful? Then there's Ricky, and he's such a great kid, and I know you teased me about setting them up so many years ago, but I know they'd be so good together if she could see him for the young man he is instead of the little boy she grew up with. I just want her happy.

Happy like we were.

Because for four beautiful, blissful years, you made it your life's mission to make me happy. Ecstatically happy. Not only that, you gave me two

41

beautiful daughters who remind me every day how blessed I was to find you.

They're the best of both of us. And I know that if you could look down from heaven and see them now, you'd be the proudest father in all of history.

I love you.

And miss you.

And as scared as I am to one day leave our beautiful daughters, I can't wait until I'm with you again.

CHAPTER 9

"And so even though our sins make us black and ugly like this piece of melted chocolate" — Gloria pointed to the Hershey bar puddle on her plate. — "when we ask Jesus to forgive our sins, he makes us as white and clean as this marshmallow."

Most of the class clamored loudly while Susannah and Ricky passed out the s'mores treats, but Bowman crossed his arms and pouted. "My marshmallow's not very clean."

Gloria stepped closer to him. Maybe this was the kind of spiritual breakthrough VBS leaders prayed for. "Well, have you asked Jesus to forgive your sins? He'll do it, you know. The Bible promises that …"

Bowman pointed to his plate. "No, not that. I'm talking about my marshmallow. It's got all that brown on the edges."

"Oh." Gloria straightened up. "Yes, well, that's just because it's been roasted, and ..."

"It's not white," he interrupted. "You said we'd be as white and clean as our marshmallow, but my marshmallow's not white."

She let out a sigh. "No, Bowman, you're right. But I think you still get the point." Gloria had been somewhat proud to have come up with a way to tie s'mores into the gospel message and didn't necessarily appreciate having holes poked into her object lesson.

"You know what?" Ricky said from the other side of the fellowship hall. "That's a really good example too. See, even though God forgives our sins, we all still make mistakes sometimes, right?"

Apparently, the children could relate to his words.

"Yeah, once I gave my sister rabbit food and told

her it was cereal."

"That's nothing. I told my cousin that unless he licked everyone's spoons when he was helping my Grandma set the table Christmas Eve that Santa wouldn't come and visit."

"Well, once I tricked my brother into putting on red lipstick and kissing all of my dad's work shirts on the collar because I seen someone do that in a movie once."

It was right then Derek poked his head inside. Perfect timing. "Hey, it's starting to rain out there. It's making the grass pretty slippery to run in. Mind if we share the space?"

Gloria tried to hide her displeasure. Her morning had been so hectic she hadn't even noticed the change in the weather. "Come on in." She hoped nobody could hear the irritation in her voice. She really needed to talk to Joy again. What was the point of holding VBS at a larger church if it ended up giving teachers less room to work with?

It must have been her lucky day because Derek

brought in the third and fourth graders, the largest class by far. Ricky and Susannah had already started scooting the snack tables back to clear a small space.

"Ok, listen up," Derek called out, as if he were automatically in charge of the entire room. "My kids, we've got the little ones finishing up their snack, so let's be real careful not to bother them, ok? All right, each side pick your medics. You have thirty seconds."

"What're you playing?" Bowman called out.

"Dodge ball," Derek answered with a grin.

Gloria was by his side in an instant. "Are you sure that's such a good idea? These kids look like they can throw pretty hard. I wouldn't want anyone to end up hurt ..."

He glanced at the tables, where Bowman was happily smearing a s'more into a little girl's pigtails.

"You just holler if it gets too rowdy." He blew his whistle, and the frantic frenzy that followed was so chaotic that even if Gloria had been shouting at him as loudly as she could, her voice wouldn't carry over the yells of the bigger kids. Oh, well. As long as nobody got hurt …

"Teacher!" squealed the girl with the violated hair.

Gloria hurried over. "No, Bowman. We keep our hands to ourselves at VBS. See, you're ruining those pretty braids."

He pouted, daring Gloria with his eyes to react.

She grabbed his plate out of his hand. "If you can't eat like a gentleman, you won't get any more treats." Maybe she was being a little terse, but she couldn't have this kind of behavior from him all week.

Susannah came up and gave the girl a hug. "Come on, sweetie. Let's clean up your hair in the bathroom." Gloria was reminded yet again of how her daughter had so much more patience than she did. *Such a good girl.* Gloria watched her daughter leave, then glanced at Ricky Fields, who was also staring at Susannah's back.

At least it had better have been her back and not anywhere lower.

He caught Gloria's eye and burst into a flame of blushes so profuse Gloria began to feel vicarious embarrassment on his behalf.

She turned her attention back to Bowman. "Well, now," she told him, "I'll expect you to apologize when she comes back from getting that marshmallow out of her hair. You understand?"

He lowered his eyes and pouted. He might have made a more daunting picture if he hadn't had melted chocolate smeared all across his lower lip and his chin.

"All right now." She passed him a few napkins. "Get yourself cleaned up. No, not like that, child. Didn't your mother ever teach you how to …"

Bowman cowered when Gloria brought the napkin close to his face.

"It's ok." Gloria lowered her hand. "It's all right. I was just going to help you clean up. I didn't mean to startle you."

"I wasn't startled." His chocolate lip trembled.

"Here." Gloria brought the napkin slowly toward him. "Let me just help a tiny bit. I promise to be real gentle."

She sighed. Had she been too rough with him? Is that why he was so jumpy?

She couldn't wait for 12:30, and she suspected that every single adult volunteer felt the same way. Well, maybe except for Derek, who was throwing more dodge balls than anyone else.

What a morning. If you were to take all the catastrophes that could occur at VBS, they had happened today. And it was only Tuesday. First was the preschooler who wet himself during snack time, then the sign-in worker who forgot to tell Gloria that one of the new kids was deathly allergic to eggs.

Then a second grader got stung by a bee, making it two students who needed the fast work of an EpiPen in one day, which had to be some kind of record in the history of Orchard Grove.

A couple boys had to be sent home earlier, but

thankfully not on Gloria's watch. Apparently, two fifth graders got into a fistfight during the games and recreation time outside. Gloria didn't see it happen, but heard the angry screams a minute before Derek escorted a boy with a bloody nose to the bathroom.

When did young people get so violent?

And now she was sharing the cramped fellowship hall with Derek and his noisy pack of dodge ball assailants. At least she'd gotten in her gospel presentation according to s'mores.

"Watch out!" A bright red dodge ball sailed through the air, straight through a window. Two of Gloria's girls screamed as glass shards rained over them.

Derek blew his whistle. "Time out!"

Gloria was already with her students, soothing fears and checking for injuries.

"Nobody move!" she shouted.

Ricky was beside her, gently removing glass pieces from one of the girls' shoulders. Derek came up sheepishly behind. "What can I do?"

"Don't you think you've done enough?" Gloria hissed. She hadn't meant to sound so angry. But what had he been thinking? Rain or no rain, dodge ball wasn't the kind of game you could play inside, especially not with kids this little around.

Thankfully, nobody was hurt, but the two girls who'd been under the window were both crying, more frightened than anything else. Susannah had come back from the bathroom and was comforting one while Ricky took care of the other. Gloria straightened up and glowered at Derek.

"I guess we were getting a little too rowdy," he admitted.

She didn't even have the words for him. "If you're going to stay in here, please find something calm and safe to do with your class." It took all her self-control to keep her voice steady.

Derek walked slowly away, and she turned with a huff to go off in search of a broom.

CHAPTER 10

"Would you like me to drive you home?" Ricky stared at the ground and shifted his weight from one foot to the other while he mumbled his offer.

Gloria glanced at her daughter who was wiping graham cracker crumbs off the tables. "That's all right. I'll just ride home with Mom and see you tomorrow."

Ricky couldn't seem to decide if he wanted to stand on his left foot, his right foot, or both at the same time. "Oh. All right."

Gloria was busy checking the floor for any pieces of glass they'd missed while cleaning up earlier. "You two can go on ahead. I don't mind."

Susannah acted like she didn't hear. Gloria

plastered on a smile and straightened up to address Ricky. "Well, thanks again for your fine help today, young man." She wondered if he ever got dizzy shuffling around as much as he did. She was nearly seasick just from watching him.

"Yeah, umm, ok. No problem." His hand raised awkwardly, as if he was unsure if he should wave goodbye or extend it for a handshake or scratch behind his ear, which is eventually what he settled on. "So I'll see you two tomorrow."

Gloria gave her daughter a nudge before Susannah looked up from the table long enough to say, "See you later, Ricky."

His face lit in a beam, and he charged ahead, nearly plowing into the door before he realized it was the kind you had to pull, not push.

Once certain he was beyond earshot, Gloria whispered, "You should have let him take you home. It's going to take forever to get all this glass cleaned up."

Susannah rolled her eyes. "Mom." It was

enough. Gloria swallowed the words she wanted to say. If God had plans for Susannah and Ricky Fields to get together, he would show them both in his good time. It was hard to be patient though, which given her history was perhaps understandable. She and Stan had met at a church picnic. Three months later they were engaged. Two months later they were husband and wife.

Oh, Stan ...

At times like this, she sounded so old, even to herself. The idea was preposterous. Some might call her middle-aged, but if she lived past ninety-five like both of her grandmothers and one of her grandfathers, she was still a few years shy of the halfway point. Of course, she and Stan had started early. Gotten married early, begun a family early ...

And he had died early.

It still sounded so foreign in her mind.

My husband is dead.

They'd had so many dreams. Dreams of serving God, enjoying life, growing old together. Of course, if Stan had survived, they would have needed to adjust at least some of those plans. She'd lost him while the doctors were still testing to find out what was wrong with Kitty. Cerebral palsy was the diagnosis pronounced a few months after the funeral.

But he would have been such a good father. Sometimes she dreamed that he was there, helping out with Kitty's day-to-day care, singing songs to her in his deep bass that Gloria loved so much, humming *My Girl* while he helped change Kitty's bedsheets or transfer her into her wheelchair.

The simple things. Wasn't that how people described losing a loved one? *It's the simple things you miss the most.*

Out of everything, Gloria missed his laughter. Ironic, really, since most of the short few years they had together, she couldn't figure out why he didn't take life more seriously.

When was the last time anyone had made Gloria laugh?

She dragged her broom across the floor, her eyes peeled to the ground for any shining glints of leftover glass she'd missed in the previous ten sweeps. What would she do if God gave her one more day with Stan? One more day to tell him how much she loved him, how she never stopped thinking about him?

One more day to tell him that she still hadn't learned to laugh since he'd been gone.

Could her own loneliness explain how eager she was to see her daughter find her lifemate? Ricky was … Well, Ricky still had some growing up to do. Gloria just had to be patient and wait.

Why do you always meddle? She could almost hear her husband teasing her. He'd been gone for so long, but his voice was still there in her head. For the first few years, she'd worried she'd forget the sound entirely, but it recurred to her so often during her thoughts by day and her dreams by night. She knew now that wherever she went, however old she got, Stan's good-natured jokes would always play in her mind.

She sighed. *If only* ...

"Did you hear that?" Susannah looked up from her work.

"What is it, dear?"

"I think it's coming from the bathroom."

Gloria strained her ears and heard a muffled sound from the boys' bathroom. "I'll go check." She left her rag on the table and bustled down the hall. Very few things could incite her to run these days, but the sound of a crying child could bring her close.

She knocked on the door to the boys' room. "Someone in here?" she asked, nudging the door open with her foot.

Keeping her eyes peeled to the floor, she made sure there were no feet standing by the urinals. Safe.

"I'm going to come in and make sure everything's ok, all right?"

There was only one stall, and tiny tennis shoes swung down below the edge of the stall door. She knocked and found it unlocked.

"Bowman? Is that you?"

The young boy, his face still covered in melted s'mores, was rubbing his eyes and trying to look tough, which was hard to do when he was sitting on the toilet fully clothed.

"So there you are." She tried to make her voice sound cheerful. "Why haven't you gone home? Isn't your mom here?"

Bowman blinked up at her. His eyes were red, his face covered in tear-streaked chocolate, but she resisted the urge to grab some toilet paper and start wiping his face.

"Did she forget?" Gloria asked. "Should we give her a call?"

"Bowman!" The angry voice made the child jump to his feet. He stared at Gloria with wide eyes. "Bowman!" the man repeated.

"Is that your dad?" Gloria asked.

He nodded but refused to meet her gaze.

"Is he here to pick you up?"

Another nod, even slighter this time.

"You in here?" The bathroom door burst open, slamming into the door jamb and making Bowman flinch.

Gloria straightened up and backed out of the stall. "We're right here. Just getting cleaned up." She smiled and sized up the man standing in front of the mirror, his hands in fists, his brows knit tight.

He stormed past Gloria, who was forced to press up against the wall to avoid a head-on collision. Slamming the stall door open, he demanded, "What are you doing in here, boy? I told you ten minutes ago it was time to leave."

"I had to go potty."

Gloria had never once been in the men's room with another adult before, but she swallowed down her own discomfort. "It's my fault, I'm afraid. Bowman got some chocolate on his face, and I was going to help him get cleaned up." She reached for a few paper towels as if that might somehow make her statement closer to the truth than it really was.

"Get up." Bowman's father grabbed him by the

59

shoulder, almost slamming him into the wall as he yanked him to his feet. "Come on, boy. I've got better things to do than stand around here waiting on you."

Gloria cleared her throat. "Thanks for coming today, Bowman." She was trying so hard to overcompensate for his father's ill-humor that she sounded like a prattling idiot even to herself.

Not that it mattered. Bowman refused to meet her eyes, and his father ignored her completely as he shoved his son past her and out the bathroom door.

What an unpleasant man, she thought to herself and then noticed marshmallow smears on the toilet seat. She didn't know if Bowman had been the culprit or not, but she made a mental note to never make s'mores for VBS again as she knelt down to clean up the mess.

CHAPTER 11

About twenty minutes later, the boys' bathroom was shining and spotless. Gloria hadn't meant to spend so much time in there, but once she started cleaning, it was difficult to stop. More of a compulsion, really, a habit that had only grown stronger as Kitty's health issues increased.

Gloria couldn't find a way to help her daughter walk or talk or feed herself, but she could bleach a bathtub until it literally sparkled in the light. She couldn't keep Kitty from coming down with pneumonia every couple years, but she could wipe mirrors or scrub counters or disinfect toilet bowls with single-minded focus and skill.

If only housekeeping was able to cure her

cerebral palsy.

"Knock, knock? Someone in here?"

Gloria startled at the male voice and hurried to the door as it swung open. She launched into her apology before she could even see who it was. "Just cleaning up in here. On my way out. Excuse me."

"Gloria?" The hand on her arm made her jump. She glanced up, even though she was convinced it was not proper etiquette to make eye contact with a man you have to pass while you're leaving the boys' room.

"Oh, hello, Derek."

It looked like he wanted to talk to her, but she made sure to wait until she was safe in the hallway before she ventured to raise her eyes to his again. Her face was hot. "I was just cleaning in there," she repeated somewhat guiltily.

"I've been looking for you. I wanted to make sure those two little girls were all right after what happened with that window."

She was still so overcome with mortification

after running into him in the men's room that she all but forgot how icily she had treated him earlier. "Yes, thank God, they're both fine. Nothing to worry about. I guess kids will be kids." She gave a half-hearted laugh.

"I told Joy about the window. Let her know it was entirely my fault." He cocked a smile. "Thankfully, I'm pretty good friends with one of the deacons here, and as rumor has it, he's pretty handy with tools. I wouldn't be surprised if that window's replaced by the end of the week."

"I'm glad to hear it." She glanced over Derek's shoulder. Susannah was coming down the hall, but when she saw the two of them, she smiled, spun around, and hurried away.

What was that all about?

"Well." Derek cleared his throat. "I know today was a little more hectic than you were probably hoping for. And a lot of that's my fault. So I wanted to know if you'd let me make it up to you. Take you out for lunch maybe?"

Even though she recognized that now was the appropriate time to give some sort of a response, no words would come.

"Or maybe you want to take some time to think about it?" he prodded.

"Yes, I mean maybe. Not right now, I better say. It's …" She let out her breath, clearly defeated. "I'm a widow."

I'm a widow? What had she been thinking? How in the world was that the appropriate reply?

"I know. Your daughter told me."

"Susannah?" So that would explain the ridiculous grin and turning in the other direction. The puzzle pieces began slowly settling into place. Now it was Gloria's turn to clear her throat. What an unappealing habit. "Listen, that's very sweet of you to ask, but the window didn't hurt anybody when it broke, and you say it's going to be replaced right away, so I really don't think that's necessary."

How did they say it in the sports world? *No harm, no foul.*

"Ok, well, I guess I'll see you tomorrow then."

The disappointment in his eyes made her wonder for a second if she'd misunderstood something. For a moment, she thought she better say something else, but instead she just stood in the hallway, watching him walk away and wondering why she felt so heavyhearted.

CHAPTER 12

"Oh my gosh, Mom." Susannah rushed over when Gloria finally made her way back to the kitchen. "You need to tell me everything. What'd you and Derek talk about? What did he say?"

Gloria's mental heaviness and physical exhaustion left no room for this kind of gossip. "First of all, don't say *gosh*. That's a euphemism, and it's crass."

"Sorry." Susannah hurried through her apology then added, "But what happened with Derek? I think he likes you."

If Gloria were twenty years younger, this might have been fun, giggling about boys, speculating about the future. Now, the conversation just made her tired. "Don't go getting ideas into your head."

"But he was asking all about you, what your hobbies are, how long you've been a Christian. He even asked what restaurants you like. He's totally into you."

Gloria smiled, not at the thought that she might have an admirer after all these years, but because her daughter was acting so invested and concerned. It was cute in its own way.

See, Stan, I told you she was growing up.

Glancing around the kitchen, Gloria did a quick inventory. Not a whole lot left to clean. She put her arm around her daughter. "Come on. Let's go see how Kitty's morning went."

"Not until you tell me what he said to you. Do you like him? Is he someone you want to get to know better?"

Gloria sighed. "First of all, what do I know about him besides the fact that he attends Valley Tabernacle and runs the games for VBS? Nothing. Is he divorced? Single? Widowed?"

"Single," Susannah answered. "I asked already. Single, never married."

Gloria tried not to let her daughter sense her discomfort. "Well, then. The next thing I'd need to know …"

"He's been a Christian since he was twenty-one," Susannah interrupted. "Got saved his junior year of college."

"And what about …"

"And he loves kids, teaches Sunday school here every week, works for some welding company doing something or other there, and lives a few blocks away from here. I'm sorry I forgot to find out if he smokes or drinks, but tomorrow that will be the first thing I ask."

"You'll do no such thing." Gloria tried to mask her embarrassment with humor. "After you put him through an inquisition like that, I'm surprised he even found the courage to ask me out at all."

"What?" Susannah's eyes widened, and Gloria realized she'd made a mistake. "He asked you out?

Already? Why didn't you tell me that to begin with? What'd you say? When's the date?"

Her daughter might be enjoying this little chat, but Gloria certainly wasn't. She bustled ahead, turning off the fellowship hall lights behind her. "First of all, I'd expect by now that you'd understand how serious it is to agree to date someone. It's not something you just agree to without a good deal of prayer."

Susannah paused with her hand on the exit door. "Well, what about when you told me to go out with Ricky if he asked? It wasn't like you expected me to put him off and lock myself in my room for two weeks praying for the answer."

As sweet and angelic as she was, Susannah could show her strong-willed side every now and then. *She got that from you, Stan. You know that, don't you? It certainly didn't come from me.*

Gloria tried not to visibly bristle. "You've known Ricky Fields since you were five days old. I hardly think it's the same thing as agreeing to date a man I just met yesterday and know next to nothing about." She tried to force her way out.

Susannah stood blocking the exit. "All right, then. I'll make you a deal." A smile spread across her usually serene face. "If you agree to go out with Derek, then I'll go out with Ricky. What do you say?"

Do you see what your daughter's putting me through, Stan? Can you hear this?

Gloria tried to look stern, but she found herself fighting off a grin when she saw the mischief glinting in her daughter's eyes.

Wasn't seeing Susannah and Ricky together one of her primary hopes from VBS week? Maybe this was God's answer to all those prayers. She might never get an opportunity like this again.

"Just one date?" she asked.

Susannah nodded. "Just one date."

"And you'll go out with Ricky? And keep an open mind about him?"

"If you'll keep an open mind about Derek."

"What if he doesn't ask me again? I already rejected him once."

Susannah's naturally sweet expression turned somewhat sly. "Don't worry. He'll ask again. I'll make sure of it."

CHAPTER 13

"Who was on the phone, Mom?" Susannah asked later that evening.

"That was Joy Holmes. I just wanted to make sure we were all on the same page about using that fellowship hall for snacks only. And if it rains again, they'll clear room for games in the sanctuary." That was one good thing about Derek's church at least. The folks at Orchard Grove Bible would rather die gruesome martyrs' deaths than allow sports in the sanctuary.

"That sounds like a good arrangement. Does Derek know yet?" Susannah asked, a good-natured teasing in her voice.

"Joy said she'll take care of the details." Gloria

focused on the counter she was wiping. Thankfully, Susannah hadn't said anything else that day about their silly little arrangement, an arrangement Gloria already regretted. She'd fallen in love once. She'd spent four nearly perfect years with Stan, and now she had his memory, and she had their daughters.

It was enough.

It had always been enough.

She put down the rag and studied her daughter. "You ok? Something on your mind?"

Susannah smiled. "I'm all right. Kitty just went to sleep."

"You're such a good big sister."

Susannah didn't answer.

"I was just about to put on some tea. Should we share a cup?" Gloria pulled two mugs down from the cupboard.

"I'd love to."

This was one of Gloria's favorite parts of the day. After tending to Kitty and the house for so many hours, it was her chance to finally relax.

73

Lately, Susannah had been joining her for her evening cup. There was an indescribable joy that came from sitting across from her daughter and seeing an adult woman she both loved and respected.

An adult woman who'd somehow forced Gloria into agreeing to go out with a man she had no interest in dating. Why had she said yes?

"Has it been a good time off so far?" Gloria asked, trying to steer the conversation clear of Derek as much as possible.

Susannah nodded. Up until last week, they hadn't been sure Susannah could get the vacation days she needed from the assisted living home. Thanks to a lot of prayer and some good luck, Susannah was free to help at VBS.

That much more time to spend with Ricky Fields. But Gloria wouldn't think of that. It was her silly meddling that had gotten her into this predicament in the first place. She should explain to Susannah that she'd changed her mind. Put an end to this nonsense now before someone got hurt.

Susannah stirred her tea. She looked so mature. "That fruit dolphin you made was beautiful. Too bad the kids who came in later on didn't get to see it."

Yes, that's what Gloria had to do. Tell Susannah the date was off. But not right now. This was the time to simply relax. Rest their bodies and their brains after a long morning at church, a long afternoon and evening at home.

They could jump into deep conversations later, all those talks about life and love and romance that a mother was supposed to share with her daughter. There was no reason to rush. They had all the time in the world.

Didn't they?

"Oh, I forgot."

"What is it?" Susannah set down her tea.

"It's nothing. I meant to stop by the store earlier. I was going to pick up animal crackers for tomorrow." With several of the VBS kids on gluten-free diets, she'd meant to find an allergy-friendly alternative for her Noah's ark snack. How had she managed to let that slip her mind?

She stood up, but Susannah gently took her hand. "I can get them tomorrow morning. That's no problem."

Gloria shook her head. "I might have to go to a few different stores. It's hard to find the gluten-free kind. I can't believe I forgot. I had been thinking about it all morning and then ..."

Then what? She'd been distracted after getting asked out on her first date in over two decades.

"Well, let me go for you," Susannah suggested.

Gloria shook her head. "No, I don't want you out this late. Besides, it's my mistake." She leaned down and gave her daughter a swift kiss on the cheek. "Be back soon. I'll put on more tea when I come home, and we'll have a cup together then."

CHAPTER 14

Gluten-free animal crackers. Somewhere in Orchard Grove there had to be gluten-free animal crackers.

It wasn't like her to be out this late doing last-minute shopping, but enough of the kids had been disappointed when they couldn't have graham crackers today that she'd all but promised to find them gluten-free alternatives for snacks tomorrow. How hard could it be? She'd stopped by the natural food pantry, but it had closed fifteen minutes before she arrived.

Which is how she ended up at Walmart. Not her store of choice, but it couldn't be helped. It was for the kids, she reminded herself.

She hardly ever shopped here, so it took her several different detours down wrong aisles before she found what she was looking for. Who would have thought that gluten-free crackers were stored with the bulk health foods, not with snacks? But there they were. Gluten-free animal crackers. If those kids only knew what she went through.

Oh, well. At least the kids wouldn't be disappointed.

"Gloria? Is that you?"

She turned around to face Derek. Was her heart racing because she was startled or embarrassed? At least he wasn't in that old sweaty gray T-shirt he'd been wearing the first day.

His smile was fresh. As if he hadn't spent all day running after loud, rowdy kids. "Just came to grab a quick dinner."

She eyed his basket of frozen meals and let out a soft, "Oh, my," that she regretted the same instant.

If she'd offended him, he had the decency not to show it. She turned back to the crackers on the shelf.

"How did your day with the kids go?" she asked, trying to act natural. The past two decades hadn't afforded her any practice making small-talk with a man she'd turned down that same day.

"They were great. That Bowman, though." He let out a whistle. "I guess there's one of them each year, isn't there?"

Gloria wasn't entirely sure what he meant, but she had her suspicions. "Maybe so." After grabbing what she needed, she backed her cart up. "Well, I guess I'll see you tomorrow, right?"

He cleared his throat and reached his hand out as if he wanted to stop her. "Just a minute. I wanted to apologize if I made you uncomfortable earlier."

Why did Walmart have to keep their aisles so brightly lit? She was certain he could see her face reddening under all those fluorescent bulbs.

"You have nothing to apologize for." She hoped her voice sounded steady and calm, but she wasn't sure how well she had pulled it off.

"I just don't want there to be any awkwardness.

You know."

She forced a smile. "Of course not." Logic told her it was time to leave, but something made her want to stay in spite of the thudding of her heart and heat in her cheeks. "Listen, there's something you should know."

His eyes lit up hopefully. She had to tell him the truth. That was the only way. She was a grown woman, for crying out loud. A little touch of honesty shouldn't feel this hard.

She opened her mouth, ready to explain why she wasn't ready to date anyone, but all she said was, "If you ever need to share the fellowship hall for the games, I'm sure we can make it work."

"Oh." His expression fell, as did her gaze. Why couldn't she tell him what she really wanted to say?

"So I guess I'll see you tomorrow," she offered.

He smiled gently. "Bright and early."

She wanted to move past, but he was blocking her way. "Well, then." She turned her cart around.

"Have a good night," he called out.

She glanced once more at his basket full of freezer meals, waved a hasty goodbye, and made her way to the checkout line.

CHAPTER 15

"Look, Dad. That's my Vacation Bible School teacher."

Gloria stopped in the parking lot. It was already dark out, and she had to rely on the voice as she made her way toward the speaker.

"Bowman? Is that you?"

He beamed as she approached. "You remember me!"

"Of course I do. Is this your father? I'm Gloria." She reached out her hand to the man who leaned against his car. Who would smoke a cigarette this close to a child?

"Kai." He gave her hand a shake that was anything but enthusiastic and spat on the ground.

"So you're the one filling his head with all this Jesus cr-p?"

She cleared her throat. "First of all, that's a crass way to speak in front of a boy so young. Second of all …"

"Save the sermon, lady. I've been hearing it all week since we took the little brat to church. *Jesus loves everyone. Jesus wants to forgive our sins and live in our hearts.*" Kai's voice rose to a mocking falsetto, and Bowman's excited expression fell.

Offering the most convincing smile possible, she lowered her face closer to Bowman's. "Well, I'm glad you're learning something, and it's a real treat to have you in our class."

His father scoffed. "A treat, huh? He must have you fooled. The boy's a demon, and no amount of church is ever going to change that."

"Please don't speak about your own child that way." Gloria straightened up.

"I tell you what. If my kid comes home spouting off your stupid Jesus myths any more, I swear I'll have to teach him a good, hard lesson, and it'll be your fault. You hear me?" The curse that followed made Gloria's ears sting with shame, not so much because of how personally insulting it was, but because she could imagine how Bowman must be feeling to hear his father talk like that.

"Hey. What's going on here?"

She turned to see Derek behind her, holding his plastic bags full of frozen food in both hands.

"It's all right," she whispered to him. The last thing Bowman needed was for this confrontation to get any uglier.

"No, it's not all right." Derek's voice was loud, carrying across the entire parking lot. "You know this man?" he asked her.

She nodded toward the boy who huddled near the car door. "This is Bowman's father."

"So that's how you talk to your son's teacher?" Derek took a step toward Kai, who was probably half a foot shorter than he was.

"Didn't mean nothing."

Gloria tried to catch Derek's eye, let him know this wasn't worth making such a fuss over. It wouldn't take back the words, and it certainly wouldn't benefit Bowman.

"See, if I were a father," Derek went on, towering now just a few inches away, "I'd make sure to teach my son how to treat a lady with the respect that she deserves. That also includes apologizing if I made a mistake. Hear what I'm saying?"

There was silence for a few seconds, and Gloria could feel the heat that emanated from both men's anger. Finally, Kai broke eye contact. "Sorry," he mumbled.

Derek turned to Gloria. "Are you all right?"

"Yes, of course." If anything, she just wanted to lock herself into the safety of her own vehicle and speed home to her daughter and her cup of tea.

"I'll walk you to your car," Derek announced, and even though Gloria tried to tell him that wasn't necessary, she felt safer knowing he was there.

CHAPTER 16

"Susannah?" Gloria asked when she got back home. "Still want some tea?"

No answer. She set the animal crackers on the counter and made her way down the hall. Kitty was sound asleep in bed. Gloria knocked on her daughter's door. "You awake?"

Susannah opened it and held up her finger. "All right, Ricky," she was saying to her phone. "Yeah, that sounds like a lot of fun. I've got to go now, but I'll see you tomorrow."

She ended the call, a look of both amusement and triumph in her eyes.

"Who was that?" Gloria asked, a sinking, guilty feeling settling in her gut.

"That was Ricky Fields. We're going out for lunch after VBS tomorrow."

Gloria sighed. "I wish you hadn't done that, honey."

"What? Is this my mother talking? You've been trying to set the two of us up for years now. Don't deny it." Susannah followed Gloria into the kitchen. "So what changed all of a sudden?"

Gloria filled the kettle for tea. "It's a long story."

"Is this about Derek?" Susannah demanded. "I thought we made a deal. Why do you think I called Ricky up and asked him out?"

"You asked him?" Gloria shook her head. "That's crass, honey. He needs to know you respect him as a leader."

Susannah rolled her eyes and pulled down two mugs. "Things have changed since you and Dad were young. Besides, it's too late now. We've already made plans. So now it's your turn to go out with Derek."

"I've been thinking."

"You can't back out now, Mom. That wouldn't be fair."

Gloria had to sit down. "Can we please talk about this once we have our tea?"

"Fine." Susannah pulled the honey down from the cupboard. "But we are going to talk about it. Don't think I'm going to just forget."

"I know," Gloria whispered. "I know."

She watched her daughter work in the kitchen. In some ways, Susannah was just a younger version of herself. Same blond hair, same feminine build. But the closer she looked, the more she could see of Stan. The quick movements, those determined eyes. *Just as stubborn as her father.*

Well, maybe that determination would serve her well.

When the tea was ready, Susannah sat down across from her at the table. "All right. Spill it. Why don't you want to go out with Derek all of a sudden?"

"I never wanted to go out with him," Gloria

reminded her.

"Why? He's funny, good with kids, loves God."

Gloria shook her head. "Those are all nice characteristics, but that's not enough of a foundation for a relationship. I hardly know him."

Susannah shrugged. "Isn't that why you date? To get to know him?"

"Dating's not a game." Gloria hadn't meant to snap, but there were so many people her daughter's age playing at love. She didn't want Susannah to follow their bad example. She shook her head. "I shouldn't have agreed to go out with Derek, and I'm sorry. I hadn't prayed about it, and that was wrong of me."

Susannah set her tea down. "Does this have to do with Dad?" she asked softly.

"What? No. Of course not." Gloria stared at her daughter. What would have put an idea like that into her head?

"I think he would have wanted you to move on, you know."

"This has nothing to do with your father." Gloria let out her breath in defeat. "Listen. Your father was a wonderful man. He loved God and his family, and the Lord gave me four blissful years with him. I just …" She stared into her cup, trying to find the right words. "This is going to sound silly to you."

"No, it's not," Susannah assured her.

Gloria took in her breath. "Well, I see it like this. And mind you, this isn't biblical or anything. This is just the way I look at it."

"All right."

"Your father and I married really young. And I don't regret that. We found more love between us in four years than most couples find in an entire lifetime."

Susannah leaned forward, clearly expecting more. "So?"

"So, I gave my heart away once, never once regretted it, and I just don't see any need to chase after a second happily ever after when I'm still so thankful for my first."

Susannah took a sip of tea. "I don't know what to say."

"Say you'll understand if I've changed my mind about going out with Derek and forgive me if that means I've put you in an awkward predicament."

"But I already asked Ricky out." There was a slight whine in her voice. No matter how mature Susannah was, she was still a girl in so many ways.

Gloria smiled. "And I hope the two of you have a wonderful time tomorrow."

Susannah pouted. "Fine. But first, let me ask you something."

"What is it?" Gloria braced herself for what was coming.

"Have you prayed about Derek?"

Gloria had prepared for multiple different questions, but this one caught her off guard. "What do you mean?"

"Well, you're always talking about how important it is to pray about who you're going to date. So that's what I want to know. Have you prayed about whether or not you should go on a date with Derek?"

"I just met him yesterday."

"Have you prayed?" Susannah pressed.

Gloria sighed. "No. I haven't prayed about dating Derek specifically, but in general, I've …"

"Then you're not taking your own advice."

Gloria felt the beginning throbs of a headache and rubbed her temples.

Susannah obviously wasn't ready to let the matter drop. "Based on your own rules, unless you've prayed about it, you shouldn't be agreeing *or* refusing to go out with him. Because we should always pray about these things first, right?"

Stan, do you see what our daughter puts me through?

"Fine." She had to admit defeat. "I'll pray about it tonight."

"And you'll keep on praying until God gives you a clear yes or no about dating Derek, right?"

"It doesn't always work like that, you know.

God's not some Magic-8 Ball."

"I know that. Just say you're going to pray, all right?"

Gloria took her last sip of tea. "Yes, I'm going to pray." She reached out and took her daughter's hand.

"What?" Susannah asked. "Why are you looking at me like that? What are you thinking?"

Gloria smiled. "I was just thinking about how proud your dad would be if he could see you right now."

CHAPTER 17

Well, Lord, my daughter's right. I shouldn't make any decisions about whether to date or whether not to date without talking to you first. So here I am, and I hope you'll forgive me if this is short because I probably can't keep my eyes open another five minutes.

Derek's a nice guy. It was kind of him to confront Bowman's father in the parking lot, and he's been reasonable about sharing the room at VBS too.

But just because he's a nice guy doesn't mean that we should go out. What worries me most is he expressed an interest in me before he knew the slightest thing about me. What kind of man stays unmarried until his age and then attaches to some widow the day after he meets her? Does it mean he's rash? Stan brought enough spontaneity into my life, not that I'm complaining, but now that I'm older, I'm even more set in my ways. I'm looking for peace and stability, not another giant adventure.

I'd gotten so used to the idea of living and dying a widow that I don't even know what I think about dating again. I've never had any interest in anyone outside of Stan. I really meant what I told Susannah earlier. We crammed enough love and happiness into those four years that I've never felt like I've needed anyone else. Maybe it'd be different if I didn't still have the girls here with me. I could see myself getting lonely then, but I've got Susannah here for now and Kitty here for good, and there's enough love between the girls and me that I don't want to disrupt that. Don't want to invite someone in who might change all our family dynamics.

And it probably makes me sound like one big control freak, but I like being in charge of my own time and my own space. I have things set up just the way I want them to be. Any serious relationship would mess up that balance.

But I didn't come here to tell you all the reasons why I'm not interested in dating again. I came here because Susannah's right. I should ask you what you think. You know Derek far better than I do. Is this a man you'd like me to spend more time with? If so, you're really going to have to work in my heart to change my opinion, because right now pursuing a relationship just sounds like a lot more trouble than it's worth. But just like Christ in the garden, it's your will, not my own, that I'm looking for here, so I'm asking you to guide me and lead me in your way everlasting.

CHAPTER 18

The autumn sun shines warm on my face. The smell of leaves freshly fallen from their branches mingles with the scent of roses. This is a beautiful garden. I can't believe we've never been here before.

He wraps his arm around my waist while we walk and leans into me. "You're as beautiful as ever."

"I weigh a lot more now than I did the last time you held me like this," I tell him, but he just smiles at me.

"You're absolutely perfect."

Just like this garden. "Where are we?" I ask. "I don't recognize this place."

He smiles, always the adventurous one, and leads us ahead. "I packed us a picnic," he says, and then we're sitting in the dirt, and he's laying out the spread. Fruit salad, s'mores, and gluten-free animal crackers.

"I've been spending too much time at VBS," I joke, and he laughs with me.

We lay on our backs, the food forgotten. Staring at the clouds, we don't need to utter a word. Everything between us speaks of love and trust and contentment.

"Want to know a secret?" I finally say.

"What?" He props up on his elbow to look down at me.

I stare into his eyes. "In spite of all the sorrow, I wouldn't trade in a single day that we spent together."

He sits up. "I'm glad to hear that." Something about him has changed, and for a moment I wonder if I somehow hurt his feelings. Did I say something wrong? I try to ask him that, but it's one of those times when my tongue feels like one huge piece of dry cotton, filling my mouth and keeping me from talking.

All I can do is listen and wait for my voice to come back to me.

"You said this place wasn't familiar, but do you recognize it now?" I look around me. Yes, I know this place. I come here several times a year. The last time was on our anniversary.

Why did he choose to bring me here?

"I thought it would be nice to enjoy the view." He sits close to me, so close that the sweat from his T-shirt makes my arm wet. I try to scoot away, but my body is as paralyzed as my tongue.

"Yes," he repeats, "a breathtaking view," except it's not my husband beside me, and we're not in a garden enjoying a picnic lunch together. I'm beside a stranger, and we're sitting on top of my husband's headstone.

Stanley Peters, beloved husband and father, now complete in glory.

I gasp myself awake, my skin swarming as if with a hundred different types of insects. My heart races erratically.

It's far too hot under all these blankets. My nightgown is drenched in sweat. I sit up and swing my legs toward the floor, searching with my feet for my slippers.

It's 3:03 in the morning. Time to make myself some tea.

CHAPTER 19

"Mom?"

Gloria jerked herself awake with something between a snore and a gasp of surprise.

Susannah was leaning over her. "Mom, you ok? Did you sleep out here?"

Gloria glanced around. She was in her favorite chair in the living room, a cup of half-drunk tea beside her on the end table.

"I must have come out in the middle of the night." Memories from her fitful sleep crashed and swirled in her mind, and she did her best to shove them out of her thoughts.

Susannah looked concerned. "Is something wrong?"

Gloria shook her head. "No, I'm just fine. What time is it?" She glanced at the clock. Quarter to eight already? She'd barely have time to get dressed, let alone make herself look somewhat presentable for VBS.

"I wish you'd gotten me up sooner. Is Kitty awake?"

"Yeah. I already got her changed, and I'm going to bring her out here to get her breakfast. Can you help me get her into the wheelchair?"

"Of course, honey. Just give me a minute to get my muscles working again." Her muscles and her mind as well. What had she been doing up so late last night? She had vague memories of making herself tea after that horrible dream, but she didn't remember drinking any of it. Good thing she hadn't left the water on to boil and burned the house down.

It wasn't the most graceful of mornings, but they managed to get Kitty dressed, fed, and ready for her day and Gloria was only ten minutes or so later than she hoped to be arriving to church. Susannah had stayed behind to wait for Ricky's mom and ride to church with him, which is how Gloria found herself totally alone when she stepped into the kitchen and saw Derek standing there waiting for her.

"Good morning." His smile was confident and carefree, as if middle-aged women turned him down on a regular basis. Then again,. for all Gloria knew, maybe they did. "Nice to see you here so bright and early."

"Hello." She offered a smile which she hoped might ease the tension she was feeling. The past twenty-four hours had given her plenty of opportunities to reflect on how blessed she'd been to meet Stan so young, fall in love with him readily, and have such a happy marriage for as short as it lasted. She'd married her first love and never had to learn about things like how to make small-talk with a potential date.

"Did you have a good night?" he asked.

She searched his face for any hint of sarcasm or anger or even embarrassment, but he looked perfectly at ease, which is why she felt the freedom to answer honestly, "Not really."

"I'm sorry. That creep weird you out?"

After everything else — her terrible dream, her long talks, first with her daughter and then with God about whether or not she should date again — Gloria had completely forgotten about Bowman's father until Derek mentioned it. "A little, I suppose. Thank you for standing up for me."

Another smile. She wondered if she'd ever felt so at ease with anyone outside of her own family.

"No problem. I just wanted to check and make sure you were all right." He glanced out the window. "Looks like a bright, sunny day. Shouldn't be any trouble at all keeping the kids outside for games."

"I appreciate you letting us have the extra space."

"It's no problem. Just let me know if there's anything else I can do for you."

Gloria's heart started to race, even though she

couldn't rationally explain why. She needed to get ready for her morning, but she didn't want him to leave. Not without …

Not without what?

You know, Stan, this was so much easier when we were young. When did it get so complicated?

Derek turned to go, but he hesitated too. Was there more to say?

He looked at her, his expression soft, his eyes full of questions.

Questions that Gloria still didn't know how to answer.

She felt her face burn and glanced at the bag of animal crackers she'd brought from home. "Have a nice morning," she muttered, hardly able to lift her eyes back up to meet his.

He gave her a nod, nothing more than the slightest tilt of the head. "You too, Gloria."

CHAPTER 20

"And so that's how God gets us all to heaven? By giving Jesus our sins so we don't get punished for them?"

Gloria smiled at the somewhat simplistic explanation. "That's right, Bowman. I'm very proud of you, young man. You've been listening." She patted him on the head while he scooped a spoonful of blue Jell-O into his mouth.

"There's still one more thing I'm wondering."

She leaned toward him. "Wait until you've swallowed. Then you can ask me."

His throat worked loudly as he gulped down his bite. "Why do people say that we're asking Jesus into our hearts? He doesn't really live there, does he?"

"Well, it's the Holy Spirit who lives inside us." She pulled up the empty chair beside him.

"But he's not going to mess with my actual heart, is he?" Bowman pointed to his chest.

Gloria chuckled. "No. Nothing like that."

Although sometimes it certainly did feel like God was messing with her heart. Like the way she couldn't control her pulse any time Derek came through the fellowship hall bringing his kids in or taking them out for games.

Or the way her heart felt so heavy when she thought about what to do about that foolish deal she'd made with her daughter. Dating relationships were far more serious than a simple dare. Susannah would understand if she couldn't follow through, but what kind of message would that give about keeping her word?

Lord, I just don't know what to do.

Ironically, whenever she'd had questions in the past about parenting or life in general, she tried to

DARE TO DREAM AGAIN

ask herself what Stan would have wanted. How he would have led their family. She knew that Stan would want her to move on. Find somebody else to make her happy.

There was more irony right there.

You were the one who made me happy. You were the world to me.

After Stan's death, Gloria began to realize how highly she'd prized him. Without her husband, life felt worthless. If it weren't for the two little girls who needed their mommy so badly, she would have been tempted to despair. Give up on life completely. It wasn't until she reached such a low point that she realized how much of an idol she'd built her husband into. How she'd looked to him instead of the Lord for the joy and belonging and acceptance she needed.

But then again, was that so wrong? God had designed humans to live in fellowship with one another. Just because a believer could live a happy and fulfilled life without anyone else didn't mean they were supposed to.

I don't know, Lord. I just don't know.

Maybe it was all pointless conjecture anyway. Maybe after her first dismissal, Derek would never bother asking again.

Now that would certainly make my life less complicated.

But she knew she couldn't count on an outcome like that. Whether or not she wanted him to, he might invite her out again, and she had to be ready with an answer.

She glanced out the broken window, out to the lawn where he was chasing one of the sixth graders in a rowdy game of touch football.

God, please show me your will.

He looked over and caught her staring. She tried to turn away, but it was too late. Their eyes locked.

He grinned.

The heat flushed to her face.

Look at me. I'm acting like I'm sixteen years old again.

Sixteen years old, never kissed, and completely boy-crazy. She shook her head.

"Well, you think it's something I should probably do?"

The small voice beside her pulled her out of whatever reverie she'd fallen into.

"I'm sorry, Bowman. I got distracted. Can you ask me your question again?"

"I was just wondering if you could help me do that thing where I ask Jesus in my heart to forgive all my sins."

CHAPTER 21

"Mom? Did you hear? Is that ok?"

Gloria snapped her face up from the bowl she'd been drying. "What?"

Susannah eyed her cautiously. "Is something wrong?"

"I'm fine. I was just daydreaming. What did you say?"

"I asked if it's all right if Ricky and I take off now. The fellowship hall's all cleaned up."

Gloria nodded absently. "Yeah. You're going out to lunch, right? Do you know where he's taking you?"

"We're just grabbing burgers and shakes from The Creamery. Are you sure you're ok?"

"I just have a lot on my mind, honey."

Susannah lowered her voice. "Is it Derek? I shouldn't have pushed you if you weren't ready."

"It's not that. It's just …"

"No," Susannah interrupted, "I'm sorry. I was going to come here today and tell him that he should ask you out again because you'd say yes, but I don't want you to do something just because you felt cornered into it. I should never have made that deal with you in the first place."

Gloria glanced out the window. "So you didn't talk to him?"

Susannah shook her head. "No. Let's just forget it."

"What about you and Ricky?"

Susannah suppressed a chuckle. "I'll still go out to lunch with him if that's what you're worried about. And for the record, I promise I won't try to force you into dating again in the future, all right? At least not until you tell me you're ready."

Gloria didn't know what to say. What had she

ever done to deserve a daughter so sweet and mature? She set down her drying towel and wrapped her arms around Susannah's neck. "I love you, sweetie."

"Love you, too."

"And you're not upset about lunch with Ricky?" Gloria had to be sure.

Susannah pulled away and shrugged. "With everything else you've got on your mind, Ricky Fields should be the least of your concerns. Seriously. It's no big deal."

No, Gloria thought as her daughter walked away, *it's no big deal to you. I know that much for sure.*

"All right. Show me where she is. Take me to her right now."

Gloria's spine stiffened when she recognized the angry voice.

Bowman's father.

"And you quit that sniveling, little sissy, or I'll give you a real reason to cry."

Bowman sniffed and stopped in front of the

kitchen door.

Kai barged in until he stood just a foot away. Gloria had to suppress the urge to back herself up against the sink.

"Hello, Bowman." She tried to smile. "Hello, Kai. Good to see you today."

He leaned over and spat into the trash can. "What's this junk I hear about you filling my kid's head with more Jesus nonsense?"

Oh, Lord, give me strength. The prayer had just enough time to escape her spirit when Kai leaned even closer.

She wouldn't stand here cowering in front of him. In spite of the horrid stench of old cigarettes, she did her best to straighten her spine. "Bowman had some very good questions today about the way to heaven, and I did my best to answer honestly."

His eyes were pools of anger. "Honestly? You call it honest to teach a little kid that we all go up to some sissy-filled spirit-world when we die and sit around playing harps on clouds?"

"First of all," she began, but he cut her off.

"Now you listen to me. You're gonna look my boy in the eye and tell him that Jesus has much more important things to do than set up house in little kids' hearts, and then you're gonna get him whatever crafts and junk he's got left here, because after what happened today, he's not coming back."

Gloria clenched her sweaty palms, hoping Kai wouldn't notice the way her fingers fidgeted so nervously. "Well now, if you need help collecting Bowman's things, I'll be happy to show you to his classroom."

She tried to step past him, but he blocked her way. "First, you tell him that what you said earlier is a bunch of lies."

She shook her head. "Unfortunately, that's not possible. No matter what you or I might wish to believe, Jesus truly is God's Son, and all the lessons Bowman's been learning about come straight from the Word of God."

He leaned in so close she could almost taste the

cigarette ash on his breath. "You gonna stand here and tell my son his daddy's a liar?"

Until now, Gloria's primary thought had been to keep the peace, to placate Kai's temper, but now she felt a flash of true fear. Susannah and Ricky had already left. All the other workers were upstairs or on their way home.

"If you're ready to see Bowman's classroom ..." she squeaked, but he still didn't move.

"Daddy," Bowman whispered.

"Not now, you little turd."

"But, Daddy," he whined.

Kai reached out his hand, but Gloria stepped in between Bowman and his father. The blow struck her in the side but caused more surprise than injury.

Surprise and just the amount of anger Gloria needed to reclaim her courage.

"That is crass behavior. There will be no hitting or striking in this building. We have no tolerance for that kind of bullying. And now it's time for you to go."

"All right. Come on, boy."

Bowman sniffled behind her. Gloria refused to move.

"I thought I told you to get," Kai snarled at his son.

Gloria knew she couldn't physically keep Bowman from his father, but she certainly wasn't going to force him to leave before Kai calmed down. "Maybe you should wait in the hall for a minute."

The next few seconds were a confused jumble of curses and disjointed events that her brain couldn't process.

She was pushed or slammed or jostled somehow.

Bowman screamed.

Kai swore.

She wanted to help but what was there she could do?

The next thing Gloria knew, she was lying on her back, blinking at a kindly face staring down at her.

CHAPTER 22

"Gloria? Are you ok? Should we call the doctor?"

Blink.

"Gloria? Thank God you're awake. What happened?"

"Derek?" Her voice was as throaty as a frog.

"Shh. Are you ok? Did you pass out?"

She shook her head, but the small movement made the entire room spin.

"I'm going to call you an ambulance."

She grabbed his wrist. "No."

"No?" When in the past decade had she seen eyes that kind before? That caring?

"No, I'm all right." She held onto his arm and sat

up to prove she was ok. The last thing she needed to pay for was a trip to the ER on top of all of Kitty's regular medical bills.

He knelt beside her, supporting her with his hand behind her back. "What happened?"

"It was nothing."

"Is it blood sugar? Are you diabetic? Do you think it might have been a stroke? Do you have heart problems?"

She let out a chuckle. Just how old did he think she was?

"I'm fine. I just tripped."

He frowned, his disbelief clearly etched into his features.

"It was that man," she finally told him. "Bowman's father. He came in here and …"

"What?" Derek was already on his feet. "Which way did they go? Where are they now?" Then he knelt beside her again. "Wait, what exactly happened? How bad was it?"

She gave her best attempt at a shrug. She thought

she was trying to convince him, but maybe it was her own mind that needed to believe she was safe, that there really was nothing to worry about.

"I'm fine," she insisted. "He didn't even touch me." At least, not that she remembered. "I got startled, and I tripped. That's all."

"And he didn't stick around to see if you were all right?"

She sighed. Apparently, she'd have to tell a little bit more of the truth to convince Derek to stop worrying. "Well, he was upset because Bowman accepted Jesus into his heart today, so he came to confront me about it."

"And he knocked you over and then left?"

"It wasn't like that."

She glanced at his face, at the stark anger in his eyes.

"Please, don't worry about me. Just help me up, and then I better get myself home."

He wrapped an arm around her waist. Her first thought was she was glad he wasn't wearing that sweaty T-shirt he had on Monday.

"Come on. Let's get you to your feet, and then you're coming with me."

"That really isn't necessary. I need to go home and check on my daughter."

"I saw her leave with Ricky. I'm sure they're fine."

"Not Susannah. I'm talking about her sister, Kitty." Had Susannah told Derek about her? Did he even know she had another daughter?

If he was surprised, he didn't show it. "Don't worry about that. Come on. I'm taking you to the doctor. We need to make sure you don't have any serious injuries."

"It was just a little fall. I'm fine," she insisted.

"You were passed out when I found you. You know that, don't you?"

Gloria was on her feet now and turned to stare at him. "Really?"

He nodded. "Now, come on. If it was one of your daughters who got knocked unconscious, wouldn't you want them to get checked out just to be safe?"

Shame heated Gloria's core, and she was pretty sure it had nothing to do with how much she was relying on him to support her weight as they made their way to the exit. "I really shouldn't," she explained. "It's hard enough keeping up with Kitty's bills, and ..."

He silenced her with a wave of his hand. "Stop right there. My sister's a doctor at Orchard Grove Family, and I'm sure she won't mind giving you a quick checkup. Nothing official. On the house."

Gloria wanted to refuse, but there was an ache in her tailbone each time she took a step, and the back of her head was tender. She didn't want to make Derek even more nervous, so she didn't touch it to find out how swollen it was, but she stopped arguing and let him lead her to his car.

He needs to know you respect him as a leader. That's what she'd told Susannah earlier. The thought made her chuckle.

"What's so funny?"

"I was just thinking about what Susannah would say if she were here to see me now."

"Oh, yeah? What's that?" Derek opened the passenger door and helped Gloria ease herself into the seat. He handed her the buckle, and she smiled at him.

"Trust me, you don't want to know."

CHAPTER 23

"So your sister's a physician here?" Gloria asked as they made their way toward Orchard Grove Family Medicine, a complex Gloria had become quite familiar with over Kitty's lifetime.

"Yeah, that's what brought me to town, actually. She got the job here two years ago, and that's when I decided to come, too."

"Where did the two of you grow up?"

"Near Seattle, but we were both done with big cities."

"Did you decide to move together then?"

"Not quite." Derek cleared his throat. "Her boyfriend is, well, let's just say I don't want to keep him too far out of my sight, if you know what I mean."

Gloria didn't know what he meant, but she figured if it was any of her business he wouldn't be so vague. "How old is your sister?"

"Twenty-nine."

She whipped around to look at him, which set off another dizzy attack in her aching head. "Twenty-nine? What about you?"

He chuckled. "Quite a bit older. I'm forty-five."

"Oh." Gloria let out her breath, much more relieved at his confession than she felt she had the right to be. "You're right," she added, hoping to deflect his attention away from her reaction. "That is quite a bit older." Heat rushed to her face.

"My parents died when I was in college, so I pretty much raised her from that point on."

"Oh." Didn't she have something more intelligent to say?

"I suppose that explains why I worry about her as much as I do, too."

Gloria nodded, wondering if that was also some

of the reason why a well-adjusted, polite, and godly man like Derek had never married. He was too busy looking out for his sister. Gloria could certainly identify with that.

"Well, here we are." Derek parked in front of the medical complex and went around to help Gloria out of her seat. She hated feeling like an invalid, but there was something comforting about the strong arm he offered her for support.

Something she wasn't quite ready to name just yet.

"Which floor does your sister work on?" Gloria asked once they got inside and waited for the elevator.

"She's up in pediatrics actually."

"Pediatrics?"

"Yeah, but she's good with head injuries. I mean, she's ..."

Gloria smiled. "I understand. I actually know a lot of the pediatricians here. What's your sister's name?"

"Janice."

Gloria stared at him blankly.

"Janice Bell, I mean."

"Your sister's Dr. Bell?"

"Yeah, you know her?"

Gloria chuckled. "I've been taking Kitty to her for the past two years, ever since she took over the practice."

"Really? Small world, eh?"

"Or small town."

He chuckled. "Yeah, that's probably more like it. I was thinking just last night about that. It's funny."

"What's funny?"

"That I've been here two years and our paths never crossed until this week. Small town like Orchard Grove, two Christians about the same age … I mean, well, that's a big assumption right there. I mean, you don't *look* like you could be anywhere near my age, but with a daughter out of high school, and …"

As much as she might have enjoyed watching him squirm, Gloria decided to interrupt before he dug himself into an even deeper verbal pit. "It's fine. I'm forty-one."

"Oh." He looked at her as if for the first time. "Really?"

She wasn't sure how to read the surprise on his face but didn't want to ask if he'd expected her to be younger or older.

"Really?" he repeated once more, but by then the elevator had arrived. Even though she could support her own weight just fine, he placed his hand on the small of her back as they stepped in together.

When they reached the third floor, she didn't want to admit how happy she felt that he kept his hand right where it was as they made their way to his sister's office.

CHAPTER 24

"The good news is I don't see anything worrisome. No concussion or anything, and aside from maybe a little bit of a headache and soreness, I think you're going to be just fine."

Gloria was so used to bringing her daughter to see Dr. Bell it felt backwards being the one sitting on the exam table for a change — especially an exam table in a room painted with ladybugs and grasshoppers and filled with little kids' books and *Highlights* magazines.

"What about pain meds?" Derek asked. "Should we get her some Tylenol or Advil or anything?"

"We could if she wants, but I'm guessing she wouldn't take you up on that suggestion." Dr. Bell smiled at Gloria, who had earned something of a reputation at the clinic for her preference for homeopathic remedies.

The inside joke was lost on Derek, who stood up from his chair and gave his sister a quick hug. "Well, thanks again for squeezing us in. You can just send me the bill, right?" he added with a playful grin.

Dr. Bell laughed and swatted him playfully with her clipboard. "Actually," she told him, "I'm going to let you out, and I'll send Gloria to the waiting room to meet you in just a second."

"What now?" he asked.

She lowered her voice. "Just a few more health questions. The more personal ones."

"Oh." His eyes widened, and he hurried out without even looking back.

Dr. Bell shut the door behind him. Gloria was glad for the privacy. Her tailbone still hurt, but she hadn't wanted to bring it up with Derek sitting right there staring at her.

"All right." Dr. Bell smiled conspiratorially. "The truth now. I haven't seen my brother this happy in years. How long have you been seeing each other?"

Gloria felt her face flush. "Oh, it's not like that. We only met a couple days ago. We're working at the same VBS, even though he goes to Valley Tabernacle, and I'm over at the ..." She stopped herself, fully aware that she was rambling.

Dr. Bell didn't stop smiling. "Whatever you're doing for him, thank you. I worry about him so much."

Gloria wanted to tell the doctor how much he worried about her too, but didn't feel it was her place.

"He dropped out of college to take care of me, you know. I felt so guilty he put his whole life on hold. I guess that's why I worked so hard at school. To prove to him how thankful I was, but ..." She stopped. Gloria had never seen Dr. Bell like this. For the past two years, she'd been Kitty's doctor.

Efficient, caring, and compassionate, but highly professional as well. This new degree of intimacy felt just as backward to Gloria as sitting on the exam table in a pediatrician's office.

"Derek put his whole life on hold for me." Dr. Bell leveled her gaze as if trying to relay a significant message. "I'd really like to see him do something for himself for a change." She offered another smile, one which Gloria found herself eager to return. "And I think this might be a very fortuitous beginning."

CHAPTER 25

"You sure you don't need any help getting up the walkway?" Derek asked after he pulled up into Gloria's drive.

"I'm positive. You've been such a blessing to me today. Thank you so much, for bringing me to your sister's, and for the lovely lunch out ..."

"Don't mention it. Now, you sure you don't want me to walk you up to your house? I feel weird just dropping you off like this."

"It's better this way," she insisted. "Kitty's window is there, and she's probably watching me right now, and as sweet a girl as she is, she gets antsy around strangers." She smiled. "Don't worry. I know my way. I promise I won't get lost." Maybe it wasn't the funniest of jokes, but she couldn't even remember the last time she'd tried to make one.

Her feeble attempt at humor at least won her another smile. "All right. What about your head and everything else? You sure you're all right?"

"I'm fine. I got a perfect bill of health from your sister, remember?"

He continued to smile, and she realized she didn't want their time together to end. "Thanks again," she whispered, which made her words sound far more dramatic than she meant them to.

He leaned forward, and her heart galloped until she realized he was just flipping up the manual lock. "Have a great afternoon," he said, matching her somewhat serious tone.

"You too."

She forced herself not to wince when she got out of his car, even though her leg muscles were achy, and she felt like she must have a bruise the size of a tennis ball on her tailbone.

"You all right?" he called after her.

She gave one last smile. "Yeah."

Time froze as she tried to read what was in his expression. She thought it was something she could name if she only found the courage.

The moment passed, and she let out her breath. "Guess I'll see you tomorrow."

His voice was soft. Inviting like a spring breeze. "Bright and early."

The entire twenty-two steps it took her to reach her front door, she was aware of his eyes on her. It wasn't until she was in her house that he put his car into reverse and slowly backed out of her driveway, finally disappearing around the bend.

"Oh my gosh, Mom." Susannah's voice in the entryway startled her. "If you're going to take off like that you really need to get yourself a cellphone."

"What?" She turned around. How long had she been standing there staring out the window? "Don't say *gosh,* honey," she added automatically.

"I know. I know. It's crass. But I've been

worried about you. Where did you go?"

"I was out with Derek."

"Yeah, I can see that. But we thought you were coming home to help Kitty with her lunch. Ricky's mom was worried when we finally got here."

Gloria shook her head. "I'm sorry, honey. Is everything ok? Did you have a nice date? How's Kitty? Has she been changed yet?"

"Kitty's fine. She's asleep. But I want to know what's going on. You took off without letting any of us know, and now you're ... I don't know. You're acting weird, Mom. Hate to be the one to have to say it, but it's true."

"I fell."

"What?"

"I fell," Gloria repeated. "I knocked myself out, and Derek took me to see Dr. Bell."

"The pediatrician? You're not making any sense."

Gloria wasn't sure she'd experienced a more pounding headache in her entire life. It seemed to come on the moment she got out of that car. She stared out the window absently, but of course Derek was gone by now.

"Are you ok? Are you hurt?"

"I'm fine. Just pretty bruised up. I think ..." She paused. "You said Kitty's asleep?"

"Yeah. She ate and got changed and just went down for her nap."

Gloria patted Susannah's head. "Good girl."

"Mom," Susannah snapped. "What's going on?"

"I just have a headache, honey. I think I'll go lie down for a spell. You ok if I take a little rest?"

"I'm fine. You're the one I'm worried about."

Gloria tried to smile, but she was too exhausted. How had she held up a conversation with Derek over lunch when she could scarcely get out a coherent sentence now? Everything would be better after a nap.

She passed her daughter and headed down the hall. "I'm just going to rest for a minute. You wake me up if you need me, all right?"

She plodded into her room, groaned as she lowered herself into bed, and was asleep a few minutes later.

CHAPTER 26

"Mom?"

Gloria opened her eyes as the afternoon sun cast long shadows through the slats of her blinds.

She sat up, keenly aware of how every muscle in her body ached.

"Mom?" Susannah knocked timidly and stepped inside. "How are you feeling?"

She looked at the clock. How long had she been napping?

"Are you all right?" Susannah's voice was full of worry.

Gloria nodded, ignoring the dull throbbing between her temples. At least it wasn't as bad as it had been when she laid down. "I'm doing fine. Just needed to catch up on my sleep."

Susannah stared, her eyes full of unasked questions.

"I'm all right," Gloria assured her and stifled a groan as she got up out of bed. A little sore, a little bruised, but she was better than she'd been at the doctor's, and she had absolutely no reason to complain. "What have you been up to? Are you enjoying your afternoon?"

Susannah shrugged. "Kitty had some trouble with her snack. I think it's been hard on her with us both gone in the mornings. She's getting stressed."

Gloria sighed. "I know. Where is she now?"

"I just changed her sheets and got her back into bed."

"You should have gotten me up. I could have helped you."

Susannah smiled. "It's fine. Really."

Gloria tucked in her blouse and straightened her hair, then glanced at herself in the bedroom mirror. *What a mess.* Oh, well. It's not like her daughters cared how she looked. With a sigh, she stepped down the hall and into Kitty's room.

"How's my girl doing today?" she asked, hoping her voice sounded cheerful enough to belie the exhaustion she felt.

Kitty was pointing at her clock on the nightstand. "What do you want?" Gloria asked. "Is it time for *Odyssey* already?"

Kitty slapped her thigh in excitement, and Gloria stepped forward to turn on the radio. While the show's host welcomed everybody listening, Kitty let out a laugh. Gloria sat down on the side of her bed, mindlessly rubbing Kitty's back.

Oh, Stan, remember when we used to listen to this show when the girls were so little? How they'd cuddle up with us on the couch? Or sometimes you'd build them a fort out of sheets and let them listen out in the living room while you and I had our own little naptime together.

I miss those times. I really do.

We've been through so much as a family, and

these radio dramas have been right there with us. You should have listened to Susannah cry at one of the episodes. It was about a year after you went home to be with the Lord, and the show was about a young girl who passed away after a battle with cancer. I have to admit, I got choked up with that one too.

But for some reason, it was nothing compared to the reunion episode they did a few months ago. They brought back some of the kids who'd been on the show from the very beginning, all grown up now, and there was a cute little romance to it, and all I could do was sit and sob. To this day, I don't know why it got me so choked up. It was just so beautiful and pure and sweet, and I felt like I'd watched these kids grow up, and now I just want to see our own girls settled and happy.

I know Kitty won't ever get married, and maybe that makes it harder for me to wait for God to bring the right man into Susannah's life. There's nothing worse than worrying about your children, Stan. Except for losing you, of course. But even then, I spent those first few years focusing so much about keeping their little worlds spinning that I'm not sure I really acknowledged my own grief until later. I was so busy helping them come to terms with losing their daddy that I didn't take the time to think about the fact that I'd buried my husband.

My first love.

Our marriage wasn't perfect. In fact, the longer you've been gone, the more clearly I can pinpoint the things I wished we could have changed. Could have known. Remember how we used to fight so much about the simplest things, like when you wanted to take Susannah out for fast food, and I refused to let her have those french fries?

Or what about all those fights about money? Sure, we had our troubles, but God always provided for our needs. Our girls have never known hunger, never understood what it means to wake up and wonder if there's food in the fridge.

We've been so remarkably blessed.

I suppose I should be proud that Susannah

wants to become a missionary. You'd be thrilled. I don't doubt that for a second. But you know me. You know how much I worry. There are plenty of lost souls in Orchard Grove. What's wrong with her serving the Lord right here?

I guess that's something I need to leave in God's hands, isn't it? Probably easy for you up there where you're with him every day. I'd like to learn where to find that kind of faith.

Maybe one day ...

"Mom?" Susannah opened the door to Kitty's room with an apologetic look on her face.

"What is it?"

"Someone's here to see you." She couldn't quite meet Gloria's eyes.

"Who's here to see me?"

Susannah stepped aside sheepishly, and Derek stood at the doorway, that confident smile lighting up his entire face.

"Hello, Gloria. I just stopped by to see how you were feeling after that fall."

CHAPTER 27

The next several seconds were a flurry of hectic activity. Gloria tossing the quilt over Kitty's legs, sweeping up the laundry on the bedroom floor and shoving it under the bed. Glancing in the mirror to discover that she truly did look as bedraggled as she felt.

Her head was spinning. Or maybe that was because her heart rate had skyrocketed. Hadn't he heard about calling instead of stopping by unannounced?

"Good to see you," she muttered, doing her best to lead Derek away from her daughter's room. Kitty needed her rest. She didn't need …

"And who's this pretty young lady?" he asked,

stepping toward the bed.

Kitty let out a laugh that sounded more like a snort, and Gloria reached out for a tissue to wipe the snot off her daughter's face. "This is Kitty."

"Hi." He smiled broadly, his voice full of confidence. "I'm Derek. I'm a good friend of your mom's."

Kitty snorted again. The last thing Gloria needed was for her to get so worked up she soaked through her Depends while Derek was here.

She glanced up at Susannah, who was still standing in the bedroom doorway, an apology written clearly in her expression.

"Could you sit with her for a few minutes until the episode's over?" Gloria asked. "I'll take Derek into the kitchen and make a pot of tea. If you'd like some," she added, hoping that he'd tell her he was already on his way out but simultaneously wishing he'd stay.

He grinned, and Gloria's whole stomach flip-flopped inside her. Why hadn't she brushed her hair after that nap? How much time had she actually saved out of her day by persisting in her slovenly ways?

Oh, well. It couldn't be helped now, could it? Once in the kitchen, she reached for the tea kettle, keenly aware of his eyes tracing her every move.

"Do you like herbal tea? I have peppermint or ginger or chamomile."

"Whatever you're having is fine with me. I'm more of a coffee guy myself."

"Oh." She set down the tea kettle and started rummaging through the back of the cupboard. "We have a percolator somewhere, and I think there's still some coffee grounds in the freezer."

He sat down at the table. "Tea is fine, Gloria." The way he said her name made her hands clam up with sweat.

She cleared her throat. She had to snap out of whatever fog she was in. Gloria loved having company over. She just had to get over this rush of nerves.

Nerves which were completely out of place.

"Do you like honey in your tea?" she asked, keeping her back to him while she rummaged through the cabinets. What was she looking for, anyway?

"I'll have mine however you take yours. Trust me. I'm easy."

Something in his voice made her turn to face him, and this time his smile filled her with peace instead of shooting waves of nervous energy throughout her entire body.

"Ok, then." He hadn't taken his eyes off her, and flustered from the intense scrutiny, she turned back around. "Susannah? Want to have a cup with us?" she called out.

"No," came the answer from the bedroom. "I think Kitty and I are going to put on some tapes and listen to a few old episodes once this one's over."

Great. She could have really used some help right now to keep up the conversation. What did they call that in the dating world? A wingman?

She could certainly use one of those right about now.

The tea kettle whistled behind her, and she turned around, startled.

"Can I give you a hand with anything?" Derek asked.

She didn't need a hand. What she needed was her brain to start functioning again.

If Stan could see me right now.

She carried the two mugs of tea over to the table, making her best effort to calm her racing heart.

She and Derek had already spent over an hour together after VBS, first visiting his sister in her office and then grabbing a quick lunch at The Creamery. The fact that he'd stopped by unannounced while she was wearing the wrinkled clothes she'd napped in shouldn't matter. It wasn't enough to stop them from enjoying an afternoon cup together.

She'd learned quite a bit about him today. About how he'd moved to Orchard Grove to watch over his sister, how he'd put his life on hold to take care of her and see her through medical school.

But there was still so much she didn't know. Last night when they'd run into each other at Walmart, they were practically strangers, and not necessarily the likeliest pair at that. She smiled to herself when she remembered her somewhat uncouth reaction after seeing all those frozen meals in his basket. Then again, if he spent his days working and his free time worrying over Dr. Bell, what time did that leave him for things like home-cooked meals?

When was the last time he'd sat down to dinner prepared on a stovetop and not in a factory?

She hadn't even touched her drink before asking, "Are you busy tonight? The girls and I would love to have you stay for dinner."

He gulped down his first sip of tea. She'd forgotten to warn him how hot it would be. Oops.

"Beef stroganoff." She smiled, not only because she was over forty years old and had for the very first time asked someone out on a date, but also because the joy she saw in his eyes matched the growing feeling of fulness in her own heart.

"I'd love to," he answered. "If you're sure it's no trouble."

"No trouble." She buried her face in her mug so he couldn't see how silly her grin looked. She glanced up at him over the top of her cup and mumbled through the steam, "No trouble at all."

CHAPTER 28

"Oh my gosh, Mom," Susannah gushed exactly two seconds after Gloria told Derek good-night and shut the front door.

Before Gloria could correct her daughter's crass choice of words, Susannah jumped into a series of excited questions.

"Do you know what time it is? Did you have any clue how long you spent talking after dinner? What on earth did you find to talk about? Do you like him? Last I heard, you didn't even want to let him take you out for lunch."

Gloria walked down toward her room, pausing at Kitty's door once to make sure she was asleep.

Susannah followed her like a lost puppy.

A lost puppy with a very inquisitive personality.

"Do you feel like you guys hit it off? Do you think you'll spend more time together the rest of the week? And you never even told me what happened at church, how you hit your head. Come on. We absolutely have to talk."

Gloria lowered herself onto her mattress, and Susannah pulled the rocking chair up beside her. "You're not going to sleep yet. You know that, right? If you can yak five hours straight with some guy you just met, you can spend five or ten minutes with your own daughter. Start at the beginning. I want to know everything."

As exhausted as she was, Gloria was thankful to have someone to talk to, someone who could help her process through everything she'd been thinking and feeling about Derek. She told Susannah everything, starting at the run-in with Bowman's father, the trip to see Dr. Bell, their quick lunch out, and then their evening together at home.

Their very long evening together at home.

"I don't know where the time went," Gloria confessed. "One minute we were getting ready to drink our tea, then I asked him to stay, and ..."

"Wait, isn't that crass? What happened to letting the man always feel like you respect him as the leader?" Susannah interrupted. A playful smile lit up her features. She grew more and more beautiful every day.

"I hear times are changing," Gloria joked. It was nice to share a laugh with her daughter.

Nice to have something they could talk about besides Kitty's health or Susannah's work at the assisted living home.

All in all, it was nice to have a daughter like Susannah. Period.

"And now I've talked your ear off," Gloria said, "but you still haven't told me about your time with Ricky. How did your date go?" She could read her daughter's subtle change in mood in an instant. "What happened?"

Susannah shook her head. "You know how I

gave you a hard time last night because you were going to turn Derek down without praying about it at all?"

"Yeah." Gloria didn't know for sure where her daughter was going, but guessed from Susannah's serious tone it wasn't going to be good news.

"Well, I actually got kind of convicted about it. I hadn't been praying about Ricky either. So I did."

"And?"

Susannah sighed. "And he's not for me, Mom. I know that's disappointing to you, and maybe things will change sometime in the future, but the more I prayed about it, the more I realized that these thoughts I've had about going to the mission field aren't going away. It's not just some little-girl fantasy I'm holding onto. This is my calling. And Ricky, well, we even talked about it today at lunch."

"You did?"

"Yeah. And he has no desire whatsoever to ever leave Orchard Grove. And that's perfect for him, but ..."

Gloria felt the heaviness that permeated the space between her and her daughter. "But it's not for you," she finished.

Susannah nodded. "I hope you're not upset."

"Upset that my daughter wants to commit her life to serving my Lord and Savior?" She forced a smile. "Not at all, honey."

"And what about Ricky?"

Gloria shook her head. "Ricky's a great guy, and I have to admit that I would love to see you two together, but that's selfishness on my part. I want you to stay here. No matter where God calls you, I'm going to support you a hundred percent, and I'm going to pray my head off for you every night and every day. But in the flesh, I want you here with me. You're my …" She swallowed down the lump in her throat. "You're a very good friend to me. Not just my daughter. And I love you, and it just rips my heart out to think of you somewhere on the other side of the world where I can't keep you safe. Because I know you're a young woman, but in my heart you still feel just like my little itty-bitty baby girl."

She sniffed and stared past her daughter's shoulder while Susannah leaned over to wrap her in a hug.

"I'm always going to be your baby girl, and I'm always going to be your friend, too. And don't worry. It's not like I'm jumping on an airplane and leaving tomorrow. But it does mean that unless God completely changes Ricky's mind about missions, there's not going to be any future between us. I told him that too, and even though he understood, it probably hurt his feelings a little. I just want you to know though so you don't feel like you have to keep trying to set us up. All right?"

She nodded. "All right." Letting out her breath, she gave her daughter one last hug for the night. "And now we both better get to bed. It's been years since I've stayed up this late, and tomorrow will be here before we know it."

"Bright and early." Susannah grinned and gave

Gloria's cheek a kiss. "Good night, Mom. I love you."

"I love you, too." Gloria held onto her hand as if that was the only link keeping Susannah from flying off to the ends of the earth, never to return to her again. "And no matter what happens, I want you to know that I'm very, very proud of you."

CHAPTER 29

Gloria was busy spreading peanut butter on celery sticks when a cheerful greeting made her jump. "Good morning, beautiful."

She turned to see Derek in the kitchen doorway, grinning widely as usual and holding out a beautiful bouquet of dahlias, tulips, and freesias. "I saw these on my way to VBS and said to myself, *Now there's something I should get for Gloria because they're* almost *as beautiful as she is.*"

She smiled, grateful that Susannah was upstairs helping check kids in for the morning. There was no one else around to see her blush.

"See?" He brought the arrangement closer, and the mixed fragrances mingled together deliciously.

"I thought these pink ones here would match your tablecloth. Don't you think?"

She didn't know what to say. "Derek, I ..."

He frowned, a look that appeared entirely unpracticed and out of place on him. "Too much? Too fast? Should I have held off?"

She should probably agree, but instead she accepted the bouquet and brought the flowers close to her nose. So fresh and clean. Invigorating.

"Do you like them?" He stood there looking hopeful. She hated to risk making this worse between them, but she had to.

"They're perfect. It's just that ... Derek, I need to tell you something."

Did he hear the way her voice trembled?

"Is it about us?" he asked. "Do we need to take a step back? Slow down? I'm sorry."

She reached out and touched his arm, vividly recalling how safe she'd felt wrapped in his embrace as he helped her to her feet in this very kitchen. Was that really just yesterday?

Derek was still stammering out his apology. "I was afraid I was moving too fast. Afraid I might be scaring you away, but ..."

"Will you let me say what's on my mind?" she interrupted, hoping that her smile would reassure him.

He nodded.

"Thank you." She took a step closer to him. A bold move for someone like her, but she needed his strength to get through this. Needed that comfort she'd felt yesterday as he held her in his arms.

She looked up at him. Forty-five years old, but his eyes were young. Young and hopeful and so full of compassion. She could do this.

She had to do this.

"What is it you wanted to tell me?" he asked. His voice was low. They were so close now she could almost sense each individual breath he took.

She could stare into his eyes all day. If she didn't have dozens of children to cook for, that's exactly how she'd like to spend the rest of her morning.

The rest of the week, actually.

And maybe longer.

"What I wanted to tell you was that my girls are my life. Next to God, they're the most important things in the world to me."

He nodded. "I understand." He took a step back. He was leaving her. Giving her the space he thought she wanted.

She was botching this whole thing.

"No," she said. "I'm not telling you that to make you go away. I'm telling you that because if this is really happening between us, if we're going to be spending more time together ..." She paused long enough to summon up some extra courage. "If we're going to be spending more time together like I hope we are," she added with emphasis, "then we need to come to an understanding right here and now that you'll be spending time with them as well. A package deal is what I think people would call it."

Derek let out a laugh, a joyful, jubilant sound.

"What?" she asked, suddenly self-conscious. "I wasn't trying to be funny. I'm being serious."

"I know. I know." He leaned toward her.

She hoped she didn't have bad breath after breakfast, because if she did he was definitely close enough to notice.

"Why are you looking at me like that?" she finally asked.

"Because," he answered, "I was just thinking that you have the most kissable looking lips I've ever seen."

His nose was so near it was almost touching hers. No, this wasn't what was supposed to happen next. As much as she might like the experience for a moment, she couldn't do it. Not like this.

She slipped to the side, her face flushed, her heart pounding wildly.

"Too soon, right?" he asked.

"Definitely too soon."

"But one day?" He was playing with her. Teasing.

She smiled back. "I suppose we'll have to find out, won't we?"

CHAPTER 30

Thursdays at VBS were historically low-attendance days, even though Gloria couldn't come up with any obvious explanation for the trend.

Bowman was gone. She wasn't sure if she should feel guilty for causing friction between him and his dad or thankful that at least the boy had heard and responded to the gospel.

Ricky didn't show up, either. His mom said he was fighting off a cold, but Gloria wondered if his conversation with Susannah had made things awkward between them. She trusted that her daughter had been as tactful as possible, but she understood if Ricky needed some time to himself.

Derek led his kids in and out of the fellowship

hall as usual on the way to the lawn outside, except this time she was even more keenly aware of his smile, his stare, his presence.

"You're blushing, Mom," Susannah had not-so-helpfully pointed out several times throughout the day.

"You're staring out the window again," was another comment Gloria had heard that morning on a fairly consistent basis.

By the time the kids left, she was exhausted. She wasn't used to long hours like this on her feet and wondered how Susannah managed those eight-hour shifts at the assisted living home. Maybe twenty years ago, Gloria could have waltzed through a job like that too, but now every bone in her body reminded her of how nice it would feel to soak in the tub or take a long nap.

Listen to me, Stan. I sound so old.

There had been a time when she and her husband had dreamed of growing old together. Christmas with the grandkids. Maybe even great-grandchildren one day since they'd been so young when they started their family. Stan's father was bald and pot-bellied, and Gloria had easily imagined her husband turning into his spitting image in another few decades.

Now her father-in-law was suffering from dementia, her husband was dead, and she'd spent all morning making a fool of herself over a man she'd just met.

That's life for you sometimes, isn't it?

"And how's my favorite VBS snack lady and culinary expert?" a cheerful voice asked.

The smile had spread across Gloria's face even before she had time to turn around. "Well, hello there."

Hello there? That's the best greeting she could come up with? What in the world did Derek see in her? He was so confident, so casual in the way he talked, the way he dressed. His church was known for being far looser in its worship style and even its theology. They lived in the same town, but at times it seemed as if they'd come from entirely different universes.

Gloria had never considered herself all that adventurous, but she was willing to try, and she suspected the man in front of her was the one responsible for changing her mind.

"How are you, Derek?"

He beamed down at her, then his glance traveled to the bouquet she'd set up in a temporary pitcher from the Valley Tabernacle kitchen. "I'm great. We had a lot of fun, but let me tell you, that was one hot day we had."

She nearly giggled thinking about his pit stains when they first met. Thankfully he was either better dressed or had remembered his deodorant today. She didn't mind at all when he stepped even closer.

"Did Susannah talk to you yet?"

"My daughter?"

"Yeah. Did she say anything?"

Gloria glanced out into the fellowship hall where Susannah was wiping down the last of the snack tables. "No. What's going on?"

"I'm kidnapping you."

"You're what?"

"Don't worry. I've got it all arranged. Susannah and I have been busy with the plans."

Gloria tried to figure out when in the world her daughter would have had time to plan anything with Derek and came up blank.

"Come on. The kitchen's clean enough. I'm really excited about this."

He placed his hand on her back, and they walked out of the kitchen. Susannah straightened up when she saw them. "Ready, Mom?"

"If I knew what I was supposed to be ready for, I could tell you."

Her daughter just grinned, and Derek gave her hand a slight squeeze. "Come on. You're going to love this."

CHAPTER 31

"I've got to tell you, Derek, I'm impressed you pulled this all together at the last minute." Gloria stared at the picnic spread in front of her. Half of it was leftovers and baked goods from her own kitchen, and the rest was a hodgepodge of store-bought items and a few leftover VBS snacks, but it was more than enough.

"Did Susannah tell you this is one of my favorite lookouts?" Gloria asked.

Beside her in the grass, Derek stared out over the small ravine where the Orchard Grove river once ran. It was completely dry now and had been for ten years or more, but the view was still stunning.

Derek nodded. "Perfect day for a picnic if you

ask me." He turned and grinned at Kitty. "What do you think, Cat?"

Kitty had been laughing all afternoon at her new nickname and kicked in her wheelchair.

"This is a wonderful surprise." Gloria leaned over to give Susannah a hug. "Thank you both for the time and thought you put into this."

Derek held out a plate. "Care for another scone?"

She shook her head. "I couldn't eat another bite."

"Me, neither." He cleared his throat, and Susannah stood up.

"Hey, Kitty, want to go on a little walk?" Susannah leaned down and whispered something into her sister's ear that made Kitty laugh so hard she started to cough. Once she was calmed down, Susannah took the brakes off the wheelchair and told Gloria, "We're just going along the trail for a little bit. Take your time. There's no rush."

Derek was grinning, and Gloria had her suspicions that this alone-time together without her daughters was also part of Derek and Susannah's little conspiracy. He stretched back and looked up at the sky. "So," he said.

"So," she repeated.

"I had a really good ..."

"I just wanted to tell you ..."

They both started and stopped at the same time, sharing a laugh as they tried to figure out what they each wanted to say.

"I had a really good time today," Gloria told him.

"I just wanted to tell you how much fun I had getting to know your daughters a little more. Kitty is an angel, isn't she?"

Angel. The same word Stan always used to describe her.

It was a good fit. She watched her girls disappear down the trail. "Can I tell you something?" she finally asked.

He was lying on his back now. How did he always look so comfortable and calm? "Anything."

She fingered the grass beside her. "I've really enjoyed the past few days and all the time we've gotten to spend together." She paused, trying to figure out how to express her thoughts.

Derek rolled onto his side and looked at her. "I'm sensing there's a *but* coming."

"Maybe. Not a big one, just something I think you should know."

"You can tell me anything."

She let out her breath. *Here it goes.* "I still think about my husband. A lot. Maybe even more now that you and I have started getting close."

Getting close? Was that the right way to say it? For a second, she worried she might be reading too much into it, but then she remembered just a few hours ago in the kitchen. The flowers. The *good morning, beautiful.* The terrifying moment when his face had been so close to hers.

No, she wasn't making this up. The way her heart pounded every time he was near was proof enough that whatever was happening between them was real.

Once she started talking, she knew she had to get

it all out or she'd lose her courage. "I loved Stan. We had a very happy marriage, and for over half of my life now, I've considered him my one true love."

Derek was staring up at the sky again. "Are you saying you don't want to be with me because you're still in love with him?"

Gloria wished she knew better how to express what was in her heart. *Help me, God, or I'm never going to get through this.*

"That's not exactly it," she began. "I just ... I wanted to tell you. I'm not looking for someone to take Stan's place, especially as far as the girls are concerned ..."

"Is this because I invited them to this picnic?" he asked. "I thought you said you wanted us all to spend time together."

Gloria thought she detected an edge in his voice, but she wasn't sure. She felt so timid even broaching this subject, and now it felt as if she'd made some sort of irreparable mistake.

She drew up her knees and rested her forehead

on them. Seconds later, Derek was sitting up beside her. "Tell me what you're trying to say. I'm not upset. I'm trying to understand. Honest I am."

"I know you are. The problem is I don't even know how to describe what I'm thinking. I've been a widow for so long, and that's been ok with me. The girls keep me from being lonely, and I have the memories of my husband to comfort me. But now …" She drew her legs up a little more, hoping he wouldn't feel the way her body trembled. "Susannah's graduated now, she's talking about leaving the States and going on the mission field, and I'm …"

"You're scared of being alone," he finished softly.

"I won't be alone," she insisted. "I'll still have Kitty to …" She paused, thankful that he didn't try to finish her thought for her this time. "I don't know what I'm trying to say."

"Then can I take a stab at it?"

She chuckled at the absurdity of his question.

"Go right ahead," she answered, but apparently he didn't pick up on her sarcasm.

"All right. Here's what I think's happening."

She searched his face for signs of teasing, but he stared at her in earnest.

"I think you fell in love, were blessed with a wonderful husband who left you far too soon, and you've made the most of your situation and successfully raised two amazing daughters. But they're getting older. One of them wants to fly off and see the world. The other's an angel, but caring for her is tiring, and you recognize that as much as you love her, it's lonely to think of watching over her all by yourself. And then we met, and so many things are changing right in front of your eyes it's a little overwhelming. Your oldest wanting to join the mission field. Your youngest hasn't outgrown her condition or her need for round-the-clock care. And as well as we've gotten along so far, you know I'm not your husband. Maybe you think that you're being disloyal to him to think about seeing someone else. Maybe you just don't know if you have room in your heart to begin any sort of serious relationship with everything else going on. Does that sum it up pretty well?"

As difficult as it was to stare into the eyes of someone who obviously knew her that well, she forced herself not to look away and chuckled. "Have you been reading my journals?"

His face broke into a smile, and he reached out and stroked her cheek.

"Do you know what first caught my attention about you?" he asked.

"What?"

"It was Kitty. I was chatting with Susannah at VBS, just making small talk, and she mentioned her sister at home with cerebral palsy, and it came out that you were a single mom, and I just got a glimpse of you. I don't know if it was God telling me or just a lucky guess or what, but I pictured a woman who loved her daughter so much and spent so much time nursing her and caring for her that she put her own life on hold. And you know what? You reminded me of myself.

"I was engaged when my parents died, and I dropped out of college and got a job and moved my sister in with me. And my fiancée left. She didn't sign up to become some sort of step-mom or step-aunt to a heart-broken six-year-old. She wasn't up to that. And I think at that point I just told myself, *You need to make a choice. Janice or your love life.* And here I am, forty-five, never married, so I guess it's obvious what I chose."

"But now that your sister's on her own and doing so well, you're free to pursue whatever relationship you want, right?"

He grinned. "Why do you think I'm here right now?"

She flushed.

"I'm sorry," he said. "Does it bother you when I talk like that?"

"Not particularly."

"But your face gets so red."

She turned away. There were a lot of things she was completely clueless about, but she knew without a doubt she didn't want his teasing to stop.

He let out his breath, his expression serious again. "I know you've loved before. And I'm not trying to take your husband's place or make you forget what a wonderful time the two of you had. I'm just hoping that maybe I can make you happy too. Make you as happy as you've made me."

She bit her lip to stifle a giggle.

"Will you let me do that much, at least?" he asked. "Or at least try?"

She nodded. "Yeah. That sounds like a pretty good plan."

CHAPTER 32

"So, what'd you think of Mom's boyfriend?" Susannah asked Kitty that night as they sat around the dinner table.

"Don't use the word *boyfriend*."

Susannah's eyes glistened. "Why? Is it crass?"

Gloria did her best to feign a serious expression. "As a matter of fact, it is. At least a little bit. It's not like we're two teens out necking at the drive-in."

"Mom!" Susannah exclaimed, and Gloria let out the laugh she'd been holding in.

"I'm being serious," she said, although she was certain neither daughter believed her.

Kitty let out a snort that sent formula spraying out her nose. Gloria cleaned her gently off with a rag.

"Well then," Susannah finally said once the laughter stopped, "if you don't want to claim him as your boyfriend, what should we call him?"

"Just call him Derek. He's a friend, and right now I don't see any need for labels."

"What? Are labels crass, too?"

Kitty snorted again, and this time Gloria playfully swatted Susannah with her rag. She couldn't remember the last time the three of them had laughed like this. Even when Derek wasn't around, his presence in their lives lifted their mood and brought them joy.

I'm just hoping that maybe I can make you happy, he'd told her that afternoon.

Well, Derek, you're succeeding so far.

She looked at her two daughters and breathed in fully. What a week. Certainly not what she'd expected going into VBS. Tomorrow was the last day, and she was ready for the weekend. Ready to get back into her normal routine. Although with Derek in her life now, she had no idea what that normal routine was supposed to look like. When he wasn't taking time off work to volunteer at VBS, Derek was a welder who had to get up at four or even earlier in the morning to start his shift. At one point on the way home from their picnic, Gloria had let it slip that she hoped his schedule would allow him to enjoy some nutritious, home-cooked dinners for a change from those frozen boxes he bought at the store.

She hoped she hadn't been too forward.

That evening, after putting Kitty to bed and enjoying her nightly cup of tea with Susannah, Gloria soaked in the tub and started to pray.

Well, Lord, I don't know if you're up there smiling at what's to come or shaking your head at the mess I'm making of this, but I told you earlier that if you wanted anything to happen between Derek and me, you'd have to be the one to bring it all together. That's what it seems like you're doing, and I just wanted to say thanks.

I have to confess I have absolutely no idea what

to expect to happen once VBS ends tomorrow. I'm a little worried that with our busy schedules and our day-to-day lives we just won't find the time to keep up any sort of momentum. Here I am at quarter to nine, and I'm already exhausted.

But something about Derek makes me feel young and energized again. I don't think I've laughed so much in the past year as we did today. I guess I do keep things pretty serious around here.

I don't know, Lord. I don't want to venture into an area where you don't want me to go, and like I've been trying to tell Susannah for years, it's so important to guard your heart. Help me do that, Lord, and give me the wisdom and the prudence to know what your will is in my relationship with Derek and in every other aspect of my life as well.

Her thoughts wandered to VBS, to the menu for tomorrow's parents' barbecue, to the little boy who'd been absent from class today.

And please watch over Bowman. Whatever seeds were planted in his heart this week, I ask that you would allow them to grow into something lovely, full of fruit and good works. Bless his father too and whatever's going on in his family situation., I pray for your salvation for everyone involved.

She leaned her head back in the water. She'd have to blow dry tonight, which meant her hair might be flat by morning, but she had more important things on her mind than her looks. She continued drifting seamlessly from prayer to daydreams and back to prayer again until she finally pulled herself out of the tub, more relaxed than she'd felt in months, and climbed into her nightgown to get ready for bed.

CHAPTER 33

"Has anyone told you that you look absolutely gorgeous in an apron?"

Gloria had to laugh and swatted Derek's hand playfully with her spatula when he reached out for one of her freshly baked cookies.

"Have you fired up the grill?" she asked. "The parents will start coming any minute."

"We're all set outside. I just came in here to find out if there was anything I could do to help." He came up behind her and tugged on the strings around her waist. "What about your apron? Need me to tie it for you again? It looks a little loose."

She nudged him away and returned her focus to her cookies. As much as she enjoyed his little flirtations, she didn't want him to think she was vain or frivolous, the kind of woman who only sought flattery. "How did your morning go?" she asked. "Were the kids behaved?"

"They were perfect. Bowman's back, you know."

"Is he? I'm glad."

He sighed. "Yeah, me too." He tilted his head to the side and stared at her.

"Did you need anything else?" she asked.

A grin spread across his face. "I could be your taste-tester. If your cookies are anywhere near as good as your scones are …"

Gloria moved the tray of desserts to the far counter where he couldn't reach. Derek made a motion as if he were about to sneak around to grab one, but Ricky came in and interrupted the levity.

"Sorry, Mrs. Peters. Susannah asked me to come get you. Said there's someone outside who has a question." His voice was a little hoarse, which probably verified what his mom said yesterday about him having a cold. Gloria was glad to see him back. The parents' barbecue on the last day of VBS was a tradition as old as vacation Bible school itself. She wouldn't have wanted a little dating awkwardness to keep him away.

"There something going on there?" Derek asked after Ricky left.

"Oh, probably just one of the allergy moms. I really should start making signs to let people know what's in everything."

Derek followed her out of the kitchen. "Actually, I was talking about Ricky and your daughter. The way he said her name just got me thinking."

"That's a long story," she told him, "and not necessarily mine to tell." She stopped long enough to turn and offer a smile. "But stick around long enough, and it'll probably come out."

"Oh, I'm sticking around. You can believe that much at least."

Gloria hoped he was right. She'd been thinking all morning about asking him over tomorrow for

Saturday brunch, but she wasn't sure how her daughters would react to welcoming someone they hardly knew into an intimate and already established family tradition. Besides, she still wasn't sure that she should be the one inviting a man anywhere, regardless of how many times Susannah told her times had changed.

Well, God, that's just another decision I'm going to leave up to you. That's the most I can do.

Outside, Susannah was talking with a woman in sunglasses.

"Mom, this is Mel."

She reached out her hand. "Hi. I'm Bowman's mom."

"Oh." Gloria's first thought was that she was thankful Derek was right behind her. If this woman was anything like Bowman's father, Gloria would take all the backup she could get.

"I wanted to apologize. I didn't find out until today about what my ex did. I'm so sorry. Did you get hurt?"

Gloria shook her head. "I'm just fine. Please, don't worry about it."

Derek leaned over Gloria's shoulder and whispered in her ear, "I need to take care of the grill now. See you soon."

After he left, Gloria smiled at Mel and pointed to one of the picnic tables on the lawn. "Would you like to have a seat? Lunch isn't quite ready yet, but we could have a little visit."

Even at the table with the sun behind her, Bowman's mom kept her glasses on. Gloria tried to give a reassuring smile.

"You know, Bowman's been a real joy to have in class. He's very bright for his age."

Mel cracked a small smile. "I know. That boy can be a handful though. I hope he didn't give you too much trouble."

Actually, all the trouble came from his father, Gloria thought but simply said, "No, he was a delight. I don't know if he told you, but he had a lot of questions about God and Jesus and the way to salvation."

She wished Mel would take those sunglasses off so she could gauge her reaction better, but she'd have to do the best she could with what she had.

Mel sighed. "Yeah, that's one reason I wanted to talk to you. That and apologize for my ex, of course. Trust me. If you want to press charges, I can give you the number for a cop who'll help."

Gloria shook her head. How much had this woman and her young family already lived through?

"No reason to apologize for someone else's behavior. I think Bowman's father was just a little concerned about what we were teaching. Bowman was very interested in spiritual matters this week."

"I know. That's why I was happy to find out he was finally old enough to come here. He's got so many questions, and I don't even know where to begin ..."

Gloria smiled and glanced at Derek, who was laughing with Ricky by the grill. Susannah was carrying the last batch of cookies out to the serving table. Kids were running around laughing and acting crazy just like they were supposed to be.

She smiled at Mel. "I don't pretend to know everything about the Lord, but I'm happy to listen to any questions you have."

CHAPTER 34

By everyone's best estimate, they had served and fed around a hundred and twenty parents, kids, and church members at today's picnic, another Orchard Grove VBS record. It was past two by the time the last of the students left. Thankfully, several of the volunteers pitched in to help clean up, and by three Gloria was putting away the last of the dishes.

"I'll tell you one thing," she said. "I won't miss cooking in this kitchen." She handed Derek the big mixing bowl, which he set in its spot high above the refrigerator, and then she took the baking tray from Susannah who was elbow-deep in soapy water, scrubbing the last of the dishes.

"Those burgers turned out great," Gloria said.

She was still trying to figure out if she should ask Derek over for Saturday brunch, and she'd spent the past five minutes praying he'd leave the kitchen long enough that she could get Susannah's opinion on the matter.

"Well, they were nothing like those chocolate chip cookies," he countered.

Gloria glanced at her daughter. "So," she began, rinsing the cups as Susannah passed them over. "Do you have any big plans this weekend?"

He stopped and studied her, and she felt her face flush. Had she said too much?

"No major plans yet," he answered. Was he teasing her?

Gloria let out her breath. If she was going to do this, she may as well just get it over with. Otherwise she'd be fixating on it all day and wouldn't enjoy an ounce of peace. "Well," she began, glancing again at her daughter.

Why couldn't Susannah read her mind?

"Well what?" he asked.

Gloria's face was so hot the heat reached to the tips of her ears. "Well, does the kitchen look good enough to you? Is there anything else you think we should do before we go?"

"I think it looks beautiful. You really did a great job this week. The kids loved you. And the parents too."

She knew he meant well, but she still couldn't forget those bad encounters she'd had with Bowman's dad. She'd already added the young boy's name to her journal and hoped that her commitment to praying for him and his family might make some type of difference for eternity.

"What did you and Bowman's mom talk about for so long?" Derek asked as they flipped off the lights and headed out of the kitchen.

"A little bit of everything," she answered truthfully. While kids ran like crazy and Derek manned the grill, she and Mel had discussed parenting and church and salvation and so many other things. Gloria just prayed that God could take some of what she'd said and use it to bless the young mother's life.

Before she was ready for it, they were standing in the parking lot. Susannah hopped into the passenger side but kept the door open, and Derek and Gloria stood staring at each other.

She balled her sweaty hands into small, fidgeting fists.

He cleared his throat and looked away.

"I had a really good week," she began.

"Me, too."

She took a step closer to her car door then stopped. What in the world was supposed to happen now? He didn't even have her phone number, not unless Susannah had given it to him.

When would they see each other again?

"Well ..."

"Well ..."

"All right. That does it." Susannah stepped out of the car, giving her mom a look laced with meaning.

Exactly what meaning was more difficult to decipher.

Susannah stepped closer to Derek. "Want to come over for Saturday brunch?" she asked. "I'm sure Mom would love to have you but she's too shy or old-fashioned to ask. Why don't you come over around nine?"

"Susannah!" Gloria snapped, more appalled than angry.

Susannah turned to face her mother. "What? Did I say something crass?" she asked, her voice teasing.

Gloria's surprise melted. She shook her head.

"You gave him the wrong time, honey," she said. Lifting her eyes to Derek, Gloria smiled at him and said, "We'll eat at nine, but if you want to be any help in the kitchen, you better show up before that."

Derek's grin was as wide as the ravine of Orchard Grove's dried-up riverbed. "Eight o'clock tomorrow morning?"

Gloria didn't bother stifling her giggle this time.

"It's a date."

He nodded. "I'll see you then. Tomorrow morning, bright and early."

FROM THE AUTHOR

Don't you just love happily ever afters? Gloria certainly deserves one, don't you think? But what about her daughter? *What Dreams May Come* is the next book in the Sweet Dreams Christian Romance series and will take you on an inspiring journey around the world where Gloria's daughter meets the love of her life on the mission field.

But love isn't easy when life takes a tragic and unexpected turn …

What Dreams May Come is the most popular of the Sweet Dreams novels. It's also based off the true story of how before the world of Facebook and E-Harmony my husband and I fell in love before we'd even met face to face. Sometimes (in fiction as well as in real life), dreams really do come true.

Read *What Dreams May Come* for the next book in the Sweet Dreams Christian Romance series. Use code NEXTPLEASE at christianbooks.today and dive into a heart-warming new Alana Terry romance!